THE
SHADOWING
HUNTED

THE SHADOWING

HUNTED

ADAM SLATER

EGMONT

With special thanks to Elizabeth Wein

EGMONT
We bring stories to life

The Shadowing: Hunted
First published 2011
by Egmont UK Limited
239 Kensington High Street
London W8 6SA

Text copyright © 2011 Hothouse Fiction
Produced by Hothouse Fiction – www.hothousefiction.com

ISBN 978 1 4052 5363 5

1 3 5 7 9 10 8 6 4 2

www.egmont.co.uk
www.theshadowing.co.uk

A CIP catalogue record for this title is available from the British Library

Typeset by Avon DataSet Ltd, Bidford on Avon, Warwickshire
Printed and bound in Great Britain by the CPI Group

Prologue

Rain drills the surface of the black canal. It's too dark to see properly, but the girl can hear it. Ahead of her, the narrow footpath is nearly blocked with rubbish tipped over the motorway embankment. The girl doesn't go any further. She's waiting for someone.

This is a bad place.

She knows it in her bones. She doesn't want to be here. Every nerve is telling her to run the other way. She peers ahead into the gloom, looks up at the dark windows of the warehouses, looks down in the gutter, looks over her shoulder. Her hands tingle as if they are on fire. She can't shake the feeling there is something or someone watching her.

But she waits anyway.

*

It hungers, always.

It takes shape after shape as its own, and each body it puts on is as hungry as the last.

It crouches on slick tiles above the black canal. In the faint glow of the motorway lights, it can see the prey it has been seeking for the last three days. It makes the leap from slippery rooftop to wet street without a sound.

*

The rain is relentless: the thunder of it louder than the swish of invisible traffic passing high above. The girl shivers. Water is seeping down her neck. She pulls up the collar of her jacket and looks behind her again. Nothing there. She waits with hunched shoulders and wide eyes, straining to see in the dark.

The girl jumps when the silent shape comes towards her along the footpath. For a moment, instinct tells her to run. But then she sees the face. She gives a little cry of joy and relief.

'You took long enough! What a place to meet!'

She holds out her hands as she steps forwards. It's a face she loves, a face she's missed. How long has it been? More than a year. But he's here now. He'll know what to do.

He holds his hands out to return her greeting as he approaches. They are nearly within touching distance before she can see him properly in the dim light. And then, in an instant of confusion, she realises something is not right. She knows the face, but not the eyes. She does not know the savage twist of the mouth, nor the hands that are growing black talons as they reach towards her. She does not know this creature wearing her friend's face.

But she knows it has come to take her life.

The revelation is like a jolt of raw electricity, shocking her so much she can't think straight. Her mind tells her to run, but her body can't move. When she opens her mouth to scream, no sound comes out. At last, she manages to make one foot take a step backwards.

But by then it's too late.

*

The Hunter looks down at its fallen quarry. The hunt is less satisfying when the prize is taken so easily.

It turns and walks away in its borrowed shape.

It is still hungry.

*

The girl lies by the black canal, her face turned upwards to the sky like a stargazer. But she will never see the stars again. Her eyes have been torn out. The rain fills the empty sockets until they brim over, spilling bloody tears down her cold, white cheeks.

Chapter 1

Callum Scott was miserable and cold. He sat hugging his rugby kitbag while he waited for his train, trying to ignore the ghost that stood beside him on the empty station platform.

The pale, blank figure didn't surprise him. Callum had always been able to see ghosts. Lately they seemed to be everywhere he went.

Callum clutched his bag more tightly. The ghost couldn't see him – they never could – but it still felt rude to stare. Even so, it was hard to take his eyes off the horrible figure.

It was a man, his body grey and insubstantial, as if it

had been drawn in chalk on the empty air. He wore an army uniform that looked almost as old as the half-derelict Victorian station itself, but the jacket was tattered and frayed, and covered with dark stains. Through one gaping hole, Callum could see the wet glisten of torn skin and muscle, and the white gleam of exposed bone. Below his jacket, the soldier's legs ended in ragged stumps just above the knee.

Callum shuddered. How had he lost them? In one of the wars? Falling under a train? Is that what killed him? Did he die down there on those very tracks?

These dark thoughts always seemed to fill Callum's mind whenever the spirits were near him, but tonight he would have been gloomy enough without them. He'd missed his train home after an away match and now he was stuck with a long, cold wait. Callum shivered as the wind whistled and moaned around him. He willed the time to go faster.

At last he heard the modern Sprinter train coming down the line, all bright lights and noise. For an instant the ghost's gaze seemed to meet Callum's. Then it was gone, like a blown-out candle.

The train was crammed with tired, grumpy people coming home from work. But even though he had to stand wedged between elbows and shopping bags, Callum was glad of the human company. Already his stomach was tightly knotted at the thought of the long, lonely walk down the hill from Marlock station to Gran's little cottage in Nether Marlock. Callum especially dreaded the stretch of woods by the abandoned stone shell of Nether Marlock church – the dead always seemed to gather there.

When the train reached his stop, Callum forced himself to set off down the hill, through the housing estate at the edge of town. It was getting dark and the wind seemed to whisper an unearthly warning. The streetlights were already on, their acid-yellow glow casting inky shadows up the driveways. There were never any spirits in the tidy front gardens of these houses, though. The estate was too new to have ghosts. Well, except the one house, halfway down, haunted by the little girl who had been run over by a post van – but she could be avoided by staying on the other side of the road.

Callum trudged from streetlamp to streetlamp, drawn to the pools of light. He walked slowly, putting off the moment when the row of lights would end, leaving him alone in the darkness of Marlock Wood.

Beyond the estate, the road continued on, narrowing to one track as it disappeared into the blackness beneath the trees. Hardly any cars used this stretch of road through the woods, and Callum cursed under his breath as he realised that his torch was still hanging on the back of his bedroom door. He normally packed it when he knew he was going to be walking home in the dark, but of course he hadn't expected to be getting home so late tonight . . .

Callum glanced longingly over his shoulder, back at the well-lit street behind him. A car pulled out of a driveway and headed up the road towards Marlock, tail-lights glowing red.

'Just get it over with!' Callum muttered to himself.

Gritting his teeth, he stepped forward.

It was like stepping into another world. Beneath the trees, the night crowded in on him. He looked back again. The road was empty now. He edged forwards into the darkness, stepping off the end of the pavement and on to the old, crumbling tarmac.

When he looked over his shoulder a third time, Callum swore aloud to himself.

'For God's sake, stop it!'

There weren't any ghosts back there. He knew that.

But every bone in his body was telling him that there was *something*. Something else.

Callum knew better than to doubt his instincts. He didn't know why, but they were always right. Sometimes it felt like he had some kind of sixth sense that warned him about trouble and danger – his Luck, he called it. He walked on quickly, shivering. He couldn't see anything now, neither on the narrow road in front of him, nor in the inky depths of Marlock Wood on each side. But he wasn't alone on this ancient path, he was sure of it. Something was watching him. Somewhere in the dark. He didn't know if it was good or bad, but it was there.

Far away, a long and mournful howl rang out, swelling to a deep, throaty rumble, then fading to a low moan.

Callum froze. What the hell was that? It had to be a dog. The ghosts never made any noise at all, and this sound carried over the dark treetops like the deep chime of a bell. He shook his head and set off again, quickening his pace. Gran's cottage was only a mile away. Fifteen minutes. Less, at the speed he was walking. But first he had to get past the overgrown lane that led to Nether Marlock church.

It was always the worst part of his journey. The lane was like a magnet for ghosts. Whenever Callum passed, they were there, drifting eerily through the darkness – long-dead parishioners making their way to prayers, just as they had done a hundred years ago, or four hundred, or more. One figure in a long black cloak always stood just beside the turning, as if waiting for someone. Callum had never been able to tell whether it was a man or a woman, because no matter where he stood, the sinister figure always had its back to him.

The bloodcurdling howl rang out again, closer this time.

Callum stared wildly through the trees, but he

couldn't work out which direction the sound was coming from. It seemed to curl all around him, like the thick darkness that was pressing down on him like a blanket. As the noise broke off, he doubled his pace. He walked head down, fast, nearly jogging. It wasn't a good idea to run from a wild animal, right? Whatever was making a noise like that, Callum didn't want to tempt it to chase him.

Now, at last, he was approaching Church Lane. Caught between a rock and a hard place. Between a known and an unknown terror. Taking a deep breath, Callum looked up.

The lane was empty.

Callum's footsteps faltered. He'd never, *ever* passed this way, even in daylight, without seeing some sign of the dead. The sight of the ghosts had always been unsettling, but their strange and sudden absence was worse. There was no reason for it, no explanation. Unless . . .

Unless the ghosts had been scared off by something.

Callum swallowed, his throat dry. He didn't want to think about what that something might be.

Ahead, through the trees, he could just see a pinprick of light. Home. Callum and his grandmother lived in the only inhabited cottage in a row of derelict alms houses, all that was left of the village of Nether Marlock. Everything else – the church, the old mill and all the other cottages – had been abandoned long ago.

Callum fixed his eyes on the warm, welcoming light beckoning from the house.

'Come on, not far now,' he encouraged himself.

As if in answer, a chilly wind sprang up around his feet, clutching at his legs with icy fingers. The wood was eerily quiet now. Nothing disturbed the perfect silence, other than the crunch of his own feet. And yet Callum could *feel* footsteps behind him. Soft, padding footsteps coming closer, closer . . .

He whirled round.

For an instant, he thought he saw something – a red gleam in the darkness. But whatever it was winked out so quickly, Callum couldn't be sure it had really been there at all.

Every cell of his being screamed at him to run, but

his body seemed unable to obey. Slowly, Callum backed away, his eyes wide in the darkness. He could feel the prickle as the hairs on the nape of his neck stood up. His Luck had been right – there *was* something there in the shadows.

Moving painstakingly slowly, Callum backed down the road. He was drenched with sweat, as if he had run a marathon rather than walked a couple of miles, but he felt freezing. He almost screamed when he felt his legs bump into something, before he realised that it was just the low brick wall that ran around the cottage garden. He'd made it. Almost.

Keeping his eyes fixed ahead of him, Callum scrambled backwards over the wall and up the garden path. The light over the small porch was on, shining like a beacon. He yanked the latch upwards but – oh, *hell* – the door was locked.

Callum tore off his backpack and scrabbled in the outer pocket for his key. His fingers felt numb. How did it get so *cold*? Without taking his eyes off the road, he slid the heavy, old-fashioned key into the lock, and turned it sharply.

The lock jammed.

It often did – the mechanism was old and stiff. It didn't normally matter, but tonight Callum knew that every moment he was outside the cottage, he was vulnerable. Cursing under his breath, he turned his back on the road for a split second to jiggle the key in the lock. With a click, he heard it turn. As he pushed the door open, he glanced back over his shoulder – and his breath caught in his chest.

Just beyond the rails of the old picket gate, deep black against the darkness of the road, stood an indistinct animal shape. Callum couldn't tell exactly what it was, but it was *huge*.

It wasn't just the size of the creature that took his breath away, though, nor the red glow of its eyes floating in the darkness. It was the waves of icy air that seemed to flow from it, so cold they threatened to stop his heart. Callum didn't need a lifetime's experience of seeing ghosts to know that the creature was not of this world.

For a long moment, he stared at the phantom. What was it? And why was it following him? Then

Gran's voice called to him through the narrow gap in the door.

'Callum? Is that you?'

For an instant, Callum turned to glance inside. When he turned back, the black shape at the gate had gone.

Chapter 2

Walking inside was like waking from a nightmare. Warm and familiar, Gran's front room felt like the safest place on earth. A coal fire burned in the old-fashioned iron grate, and a bunch of brightly coloured rowan berries and hazel leaves had been arranged in a jar on the drop-leaf table at the bottom of the stairs. Piles of books covered every other available surface. A creaky radio-cassette player was bouncing quietly to a big-band beat, the worn tape hissing faintly in the background. Normally Callum hated Gran's taste in music – it was at least half a century behind the times, along with pretty much everything else she liked – but tonight he was actually pleased to hear the familiar tootle of trumpets. He leaned back against the door, fighting for breath as sweat trickled down his face.

'Callum!' Gran gasped, looking up at him. Below her close-cropped grey hair, her clear blue eyes were tight with concern. She was curled in her favourite spot, a cracked leather armchair that fitted exactly into the space under the narrow stairs. In daylight, from the chair, you could see straight up the road into the heart of Marlock Wood. She often set up her easel there, splashing out watercolour paintings of the same scene in every possible weather and season. And keeping a sharp eye on the few people who came and went along the lonely road.

Callum fought to still his chattering teeth. 'Hi, Gran.'

'Callum, sit down!' Gran uncurled herself from her chair and was at his side in a second. 'You're as white as a sheet! What's wrong? Not that lad from school bothering you again?'

Callum shrugged off her concerned hands as she tried to take his jacket from him. 'I'm not afraid of *him*!' he replied quickly.

Gran steered him to the other armchair and made him sit. He hadn't even taken off his boots.

'Tell me what happened,' she ordered in a voice of iron. She didn't use that tone very often.

'I don't like that road at night,' Callum said.

'Well, at least you're safe from traffic,' said Gran. She looked at him sharply, like a ferret sniffing out a rabbit. 'Did something frighten you?'

Callum shook his head. 'A dog followed me, that's all. It's gone now. I don't know where it came from.'

Gran gave a knowing nod. 'Warren's farm, maybe, on the other side of the wood. His dogs are always getting through the fence.'

'Yeah, you're probably right.'

Trust Gran to come up with a rational explanation. She'd never had any time for what she called 'hocus-pocus'. But she hadn't felt the eerie, freezing wind, nor seen the huge black shape that had appeared and then vanished at the gate. Callum didn't know what it was, but he knew it hadn't been a farmer's dog.

'Well, thank goodness you're home safe and the rain hasn't come on yet. Listen to the wind rising out there. I was starting to worry! Trains late again, I suppose.' Gran pointed to the grate. 'Supper's not ready, I'm afraid. I'm doing jacket potatoes in the fire and they take forever. Why don't you have a bath? The water's hot, I put it on an hour ago. I thought you'd need it after your match. Go on and fill the tub and I'll fix you a drink to keep you going till the spuds are done.'

Callum smiled weakly. 'Thanks, Gran.'

He stood up again, relieved that he was no longer shaking. He took off his coat and hung it on the narrow row of coat hooks by the door, and left his boots on the mat beneath. Gran's cottage might be tiny, and the furniture old and battered, but she ran a tight ship. *As long as everything is in its right place, there's plenty of room*, she liked to say.

While Gran set the kettle on the gas ring in the lean-to kitchen, Callum moved into the bathroom and began to fill the bath. Much as Gran's fussing annoyed him sometimes, he loved this little house. One small sitting room, a miniature kitchen and a bathroom tacked on the back, two even tinier rooms upstairs: that was all there was to it. It was like a cocoon, small and safe. Callum had *always* loved it, even before it became his home. He wondered why he felt that way. Maybe it was because he knew his dad had grown up here too.

Callum ran the water scalding hot. Waiting for the tub to fill, he studied his face in the mirror for a moment, trying to see if there was anything in his own features that made him different from anyone else. But no, he looked pretty average: the broad cheekbones that Gran insisted were 'dashing good looks', smeared with mud from the match, and his tangled brown hair, too long and standing up at the back as usual. His face was a little anxious around the eyes, with a crease of worry between the eyebrows – but it was just a face. A normal face. Nothing to give away the fact that he was a freak who saw ghosts round every corner.

Gran tapped on the door. 'Bovril or hot chocolate?' she called.

'I don't mind, Gran,' Callum sighed.

What would she think if she caught him staring at himself in the mirror? That he was *admiring* himself, probably.

Undressing quickly, Callum lowered himself into the tub and tried to pull himself together. The last thing he wanted was for Gran to start digging for the real reason he'd been scared. He never talked to her about his strange abilities. Gran might be eccentric and old-fashioned, but she didn't have a superstitious bone in her body and Callum didn't want her to think there was anything wrong with him. All the things that made him different – his Luck, the ghosts – these things weren't *new* to Callum. When he'd been very small, he sometimes hadn't been able to tell the ghosts apart from the living. In the first horrible weeks after his mum's accident, Callum had tried to console himself with his strange ability. *At least I'll see her again,* he had thought. *Even if she won't be able to talk to me or hold me, at least I'll see her.*

But he never did. He only ever saw the ghosts of strangers. *And what's the use of that?* Callum thought as he ran more close-to-boiling water into the bath. *What's the point of being able to see ghosts if I can't see the ones I care about?*

'Callum?' His grandmother rapped at the door

21

again. 'Your Bovril's waiting in your room. Don't let it get cold! Hurry up now; I put the heater on for you, and you know I don't like to leave it when no one's there.'

With another sigh Callum washed quickly and drained the tub.

Up in his room, he dressed again. He had the bigger of the two small bedrooms. The one that had been his dad's, for the same reason it was now his: he had more stuff than Gran. The room was crammed with football and rugby boots, cricket bats and tennis racquets, a guitar and music stand, and a large portable CD player that had belonged to his mother. On the floor was a growing pile of books. Gran joked that she and Callum went in for competitive book-collecting.

Well-trained by Gran, Callum kept his things in good order, and by the standards of the other kids at school he didn't have much – there was no desk, no computer, no telly, no games console.

No ghosts, either. No ghosts ever in this room. No ghosts in the whole cottage. For the first time, Callum wondered why.

The wind whistled sharply under the loose tiles above his window, reminding him of the howl of the creature in the dark. He shivered. What had it been? He could think of one way to find out, but he would have to be careful.

'Callum? Supper's ready!' Gran called up the stairs.

Callum dutifully switched off the electric heater and went back downstairs, pulling the drop-leaf table away from the wall behind him. The room was so small that, opened out, the table blocked the narrow stairway.

'Better?' Gran asked kindly, fishing the charred potatoes out of the grate as Callum laid the table.

'Yeah.' He gave her a little smile.

'You should keep your torch in your bag this time of year.'

'Probably,' Callum replied. She was right about that. He wouldn't be caught out again.

Gran continued to fuss over him as they ate, giving him the two biggest potatoes and most of the baked beans to go on top of them, but Callum didn't mind. After the horror of the woods, it felt OK to be looked after for a while. Gran seemed to relax too, laughing as she recounted the latest gossip from the town.

Finally, after they had both finished eating, Callum plucked up the courage to ask the question he'd been brooding on all evening.

'Gran, do any of your books mention ghosts in Marlock Wood?'

Gran raised a surprised eyebrow.

'Ghosts? I thought you didn't read about anything but music and sport.'

'Well, it's for a school project,' Callum improvised, trying to throw her off the scent. 'On, um, local history.'

'I haven't got anything like that. There's a book of old photos of Stockport,' Gran replied, shaking her head as she glanced around at the shelves that lined the room, sagging under the weight of the hundreds of books they held. 'But I'm not sure where.'

'Never mind,' Callum said with false brightness. 'I'll try the library.'

*

Lying in bed that night, listening to the rising wind rattling the old window in its frame, Callum tried again to make sense of what had happened earlier. Something was different, that much was certain. Something had changed in the spirit world around him, but what it was and what it meant for him, Callum couldn't tell.

He shifted restlessly. Gran had gone to bed half an hour ago and the cottage was silent, but he still couldn't get to sleep. His brain kept playing tricks on him, telling him there was something moving in the darkest corner of the room. Creeping towards the bed.

Callum froze. He *wasn't* imagining it. Something was slinking slowly across the tattered old carpet, low and secretive, keeping to the shadows but getting closer and closer . . .

Without warning, a dark shape sprang from the floor, and landed on Callum's chest. Sharp claws pierced his skin and a pair of eyes flashed in the moonlight. Heart pounding, Callum scrambled into a sitting position, sending the creature flying. It tumbled down to the foot of the bed with an outraged yowl.

Callum let out an explosive breath of relief. It was only Cadbury, Gran's kamikaze black-and-white tomcat.

'Cad!' he laughed. 'You made me jump out of my skin!'

Cadbury gave his short trill of greeting and cautiously picked his way up into Callum's lap.

'So,' said Callum, scratching him behind the ears. 'Do cats see ghosts? Is that why you're bouncing off the walls the whole time?'

Cadbury wedged himself under Callum's arm, kneading and purring, as if he was trying to smooth away his worries.

'But it wasn't a ghost that followed me tonight,' Callum told the cat softly. 'Not a normal one. It was something new.'

Then an equally unpleasant thought twisted in Callum's mind. What if it *wasn't* something new? What if his ability to see these unnatural things was growing stronger?

What if the presence he felt tonight had always been there, and he simply hadn't noticed it before?

Chapter 3

Callum ran.

At first he ran for the pleasure of it, as he sometimes did around the track at school, but after a while he realised he didn't know where he was. He didn't want to stop and look; in fact, he was afraid of stopping, afraid of what he might see or meet if he even slowed down.

So he kept on running.

The pavement beneath his feet was slick and slippery, lit only by moonlight. But it wasn't raining, and Callum didn't dare look down to see what made it wet. Where *was* he?

Nothing was familiar. The buildings he ran past were old and decaying, their windows hollow black cavities or nailed over with rotting boards. He came to a crossroads and turned blindly. Any street was better than this one. But after ten metres he knew he'd gone the wrong way, and had to turn and backtrack. He didn't know where he was, but he knew which way he had to go.

He was looking for something.

Callum ran without tiring. His rugby boots struck rhythmically against the paving slabs, and hollow echoes bounced off the black and ruined walls. Nothing around him changed: same empty, nameless streets; same faint moonlight; same hard pavement underfoot. But deep within him, Callum felt a needling sense of urgency, pushing him forwards and making him more and more nervous with every step. He was wasting time; he had to move faster.

Callum forced himself to stand still. He wasn't at all out of breath but he needed to think. Maybe his Luck was guiding him, though he couldn't remember it ever driving him so hard before.

He began to run again. Suddenly now he was barefoot, and could feel the wet concrete against his skin, faintly sticky to the touch. It was horrible, but he had to keep going. Now the only sound was the soft slap of his feet as he ran.

There was a light over the streets ahead, the glow of motorway lamps, and Callum ran towards the bright line with relief. Now he was running alongside a canal beneath a motorway embankment. The light from the motorway was so far above him he couldn't see it reflected in the water. Something terrible had happened here in these shadows; Callum could feel it – hear it, like an echo. Dread filled him and he thought about trying to double back, but his internal navigation system wouldn't let him.

He could hear rain falling in the black canal, spitting and hissing as it hit the water's surface, but he stayed strangely dry. The path was empty, except for a pile of rubbish. Whatever had happened here was over. It wasn't what he was looking for. Callum ran on past the shapeless tangle of shopping trolleys and mattresses.

Suddenly he was running through utter blackness,

as though he'd entered a tunnel. It was like running with his eyes shut, but he didn't hit anything. Once he glanced up, and there were stars overhead, then he was plunged back into the darkness. Callum rubbed his eyes until red spots flashed against his eyelids.

A shriek of pure terror split the night. The noise drove into Callum's head like an iron spike. Although his heart pounded with fear, his feet and legs reacted automatically, turning towards the sound. That was the way he had to go.

But now he was in a different city. Somehow he had travelled hundreds of miles, running in the starlit dark, but there was no time to stop and wonder how. Cars lined the streets. Terraced houses flashed past on either side, charmless but ordinary.

Then the voice cried out again:

'Help me!'

'Where are you?' Callum yelled. 'I'm coming!'

When the next scream came, it was one of mindless agony.

Abruptly, Callum turned a corner into a narrow

alley. The high brick walls of urban back gardens rose steeply on either side of him, still echoing with the terrible scream. All the gates were shut and locked. The windows of the houses beyond were dark. The pavement was lined with cracks. Grey, patchy grass straggled through the gaps.

This was the place. Callum knew it the moment his bare feet touched the cool, tacky concrete. But now everything was still and quiet; not even the echo remaining.

Desolation swept over him. He was too late.

Halfway down the alley, he found what he was looking for. Slumped against the wall, hands out and open like a beggar, was a dead boy, no older than Callum. Blood smeared his cheeks, black in the moonlight. He stared blankly across the alley from empty sockets.

His eyes had been torn out.

Callum stared at the dead boy's ruined features, fighting the urge to be sick. He felt guilt slither into the hollow pit of his stomach. He should have been faster. He might have been able to prevent this.

'What happened to you?' Callum whispered. 'Why were you calling me?'

The boy's ravaged face offered no answer, his sightless gaze fixed on the opposite wall of the alley.

Callum turned. There were words scrawled across the bricks. The letters glistened against the rough surface, and Callum did not need to look any closer to know that they were written in blood.

IT IS COMING

That was all. Three words, ten letters.

IT IS COMING

As if in confirmation, a long, deep howl echoed through the night, terrifyingly close and horribly familiar. Callum spun round, pressing his back to the wall next to the savaged body as the howl reached a crescendo –

And then he was sitting up in bed, wide awake and tangled in his sheets.

The hairs at the back of his neck were standing on end and he was panting like he really had been running for the past hour. The soles of his feet were ice-cold, as if they still felt the wet concrete of the street in his dream beneath them.

He didn't feel as though he'd woken from a nightmare, didn't feel any relief from his sense of failure. He knew he was awake now, but his horror and disgust were as real as they had been in the dream.

So was the wailing howl echoing in the darkness.

Callum dug his fingers into his mattress, fighting the rising panic. Was the creature still outside? Had its call woken him up – or had it triggered the dream?

The spine-chilling cry faded to a low murmur and Callum forced himself to lie still, listening for it again. Long moments passed. The wind moaned as it rattled the window frame, but it was just wind, not the voice of some baying demon. At the bottom of the bed, Cadbury raised his head and gave him a quizzical look.

'Just a nightmare, Cad.'

But it wasn't just a nightmare. Callum wanted to believe it was his mind playing tricks, but he knew better. Forcing his frozen feet out of bed, he slipped over to the window. He didn't turn on the light – the only glowing window in the row of empty cottages

33

would attract too much attention – just pressed his face against the leaded panes.

Held in place by the pressure of Callum's touch, the window stopped rattling, but the branches of the rowan tree growing by the side of the cottage still tapped at the glass. Callum held his breath to keep the panes from misting up and stared out into the windy night.

There was no sign of the animal shadow that had followed him home, but Callum knew now, with certainty, that it was still there. He could almost sense its closeness; it could be at the old mill, or at the bottom of the hill where Marlock Road joined the main road to Stockport, or, more likely, lurking in the cover of the woods.

Shooing Cadbury out of the way, Callum wrapped his duvet round himself, up to his chin, then sat at the window staring out. Was there no place now he could feel safe, no place he could sleep soundly? The cottage had always been a haven for him. There weren't any ghosts here, no need for Luck. It was the one place where Callum could feel normal – at least, it had been until now.

'What's happening, Cad?' he whispered.

His Luck sometimes warned him about danger, but it always operated by instinct. He'd never had a dream like this before. He'd never been given an actual *message*.

IT IS COMING

All through the night, Callum sat at the window, his mind racing, his ears straining for the sound of a howl.

But he heard and saw nothing.

Chapter 4

The Hunter has left the boy behind; the one who tried to fight, even when his weak body was already dying. It was an exciting chase, briefly, but now the boy lies dead, and another victim awaits.

The Hunter begins to lay its path. It cannot smell, but it does not need to. Its victims leave trails stronger than any scent. Their own power is their undoing, calling the Hunter to them.

But something is different this time. The trail is confused. It flickers, coming and going too swiftly to follow. Something is hiding this one. Maybe this boy-child is even trying to hide himself.

Ah . . .

The Hunter cannot smile without borrowing a human face, but it feels the pleasure that goes with a smile. A challenge! It is time for the real chase to begin.

It is still hungry.

Chapter 5

It didn't seem possible that this was just another school day, as ordinary as any other. Same old steam on the cottage windowpanes, same old open fire in the grate, same old Gran frying eggs on the gas ring. Callum cupped one hand round his mug of tea, slowly stirring sugar into it with the other, and listened to the bored tones of the radio announcer relaying the morning's news.

'*The mutilated body of a teenage boy has been discovered in a residential area of South London. The boy's identity has not been released, but the violent nature of the death tallies with a number of murders reported in recent weeks in*

Newcastle, Glasgow, Birmingham, and two undisclosed rural locations in Wales and the south-west . . .'

Callum dropped the sugar spoon and slurped his tea, trying not to listen. Another hideous news story. Just what he needed after a night of dark dreams and insomnia.

'Reports suggest that these apparent serial murders may be the result of a gang vendetta, although police say that copycat killings cannot be ruled out.'

With a snort of outrage, Gran banged two plates of fried eggs and toast down on to the table.

'Detectives have refused to comment on rumours that the murderer left a signature at the scene of the latest crime, heralding further attacks. Eyewitnesses claim that the victim's own blood was used to write the words "IT IS COMING" on a wall close to where the body was found.'

'Good God!' Gran rounded on the radio with an explosive gasp of anger. 'What makes you think we want to hear all this?'

The radio went instantly quiet, as though scolded into silence. Nether Marlock was in a small valley and occasionally lost reception, but instead of fiddling with the antenna as she usually did, Gran snapped the radio off.

'Why do they broadcast this stuff at eight o'clock in the morning! Why do they broadcast it at all? Copycats, indeed! What would they have to copy if they didn't get the gory details of every crime handed to them on a platter by the media?'

Callum sat frozen, hardly hearing his grandmother's words. The calm, unfeeling tones of the radio announcer played in a relentless loop in his head:

The victim's own blood was used to write the words "IT IS COMING" . . .

Callum's spine tingled, and his heart thumped so loudly he wondered if Gran could hear it. How could he have known? Last night's events – last night's *real* events – seemed to match his dream *exactly*. A dead boy behind a row of houses. And the message in blood – the exact same words on the wall. How could he *possibly* have known? Was it some sort of premonition?

Callum subdued a shiver as another uncomfortable thought hit him. Last night in the woods, he had seen a new sort of ghost – or whatever it was. Maybe his dream was another new kind of supernatural ability that he hadn't known he possessed. Maybe this was just the beginning . . .

He slowly picked up his teaspoon and gave himself another generous spoonful of sugar as Gran made a triumphant finish to her rant.

'Now you see why I won't get a television! It's bad enough having to *listen* to such stuff first thing in the morning without having to *look* at it too.'

'Gran,' Callum asked casually. 'Did you hear a dog howling in the night?'

Gran frowned. 'Did I hear what?'

'Howling last night. Outside.'

She shrugged, still frowning. 'I don't think so, Callum. What makes you ask that?'

'You talking about hearing things without seeing them.'

Gran turned away and busied herself at the sink.

'Well I didn't hear anything odd. There was a howling gale, certainly. And when the wind gets in under the eaves it makes some strange noises. It plays up in the empty cottages too. It's like living in a set of pan pipes sometimes. It was probably your imagination.'

Callum sighed and turned back to his egg, but he'd lost his appetite. After the announcement on the radio, the morning didn't feel so ordinary any more. Pushing back his chair, he pulled on his coat.

'I'd better get going or I'll be late,' he said.

'Don't forget to put your torch in your rucksack,' Gran reminded him.

'Yeah.'

'And stay on the road.'

'OK, OK!' Callum looked up, surprised at this sudden shower of advice. 'Why wouldn't I stay on the road? I'm not going to go off into those woods in the dark, that's for sure!'

'Best be home before it gets dark,' Gran finished firmly. 'Then you won't need to worry.'

'Howling dogs can wander about in daylight too, you know,' replied Callum. 'And on roads!'

Gran gave a little shrug. 'Whatever you say, Callum. Have a good day, dear.'

*

Callum headed back up the hill through Marlock Wood. Whatever had followed him through the trees last night wasn't there this morning. He didn't hear or feel anything – no soft padding of feet, no icy breath of wind, and above all, no howling. Still no ghosts around Nether Marlock church either, but in daylight that didn't seem so worrying.

Callum paused for a moment to watch a pair of chaffinches hopping about fearlessly in the briars at the bottom of the lane.

'You're not scared of anything, are you?' he said under his breath. 'I guess I shouldn't be, either.'

Up in the town, the high street was going about its everyday morning business. Callum passed the kids in front of the post office, stocking up on sweets and crisps before the long, grinding day of schoolwork ahead. The shopkeeper only allowed two school-children in at a time and kept a strict watch at the door, like a bouncer at a nightclub. There were about twenty kids standing in the queue outside, messing around and texting their friends while they waited to be allowed in. Callum nodded at a couple of kids from his class as he passed, and they nodded back.

He got along with most of his classmates just fine, even if he didn't mix with them much. He had to keep normal kids at a distance. He'd learned that the hard way at primary school. Callum had a few friends back then, but it hadn't been easy to hold on to them when they kept catching him staring at things they couldn't see. One day, whispers started going round the playground and Callum found himself spending break time alone.

In the hallways of Marlock High School, all the talk was about the latest teenage murder victim. Callum shoved his rugby boots into his locker and pulled out his maths books as the gossip echoed around him.

'It's got to be something to do with vampires!' said one girl.

Someone laughed. 'Don't be stupid. We're not in a movie!'

'Honest. They said there was writing in *blood*.'

'Or maybe it's gangsters,' said another voice. 'A drug ring, taking revenge . . .'

The laughing girl put on a ghoulish voice:

'Where will they strike next?' Her friends broke into nervous giggles.

Callum banged his locker shut.

Hugh Mayes, a boy from Callum's class, gave his own locker door a sympathetic slam. 'Girls, eh?'

'Too daft,' Callum agreed. Gran was right about the media, stirring up rumours and panic.

The morning passed even more slowly than usual. Callum almost dozed off in maths and geography after the horror-filled race in his dream and the sleepless night that had followed, but Hugh and his mate Andrew kept giving him helpful pokes in the ribs with their pencils. He managed not to fall asleep over his books, but he was feeling pretty exhausted by lunchtime.

Callum dumped his books in his locker again after his final class of the morning and headed to lunch. The stairwell outside the cafeteria was crowded as usual. One girl, coming down the stairs towards Callum, was dressed in flowing Victorian mourning clothes, her long black skirt glittering with sequins.

Callum had just stepped aside to let the ghost float

past when he realised that it wasn't a ghost at all, just that ridiculous New Age girl, Melissa Roper, her black school uniform accessorised with tasselled Indian silk scarves and assorted healing crystals. Other girls wore foundation and eye-shadow; Melissa tattooed the backs of her hands with henna. Today she had on a jingling collection of shiny crucifixes on a silver chain. Protection against Dracula?

Callum grinned in spite of himself. Of course – it was her voice he'd heard that morning by his locker, suggesting that the serial murders were done by vampires. Trust Melissa. His grin faded, though, as she met his eye and smiled back shyly. Melissa, with her alternative dress sense and her goofy ideas, hadn't learned the art of keeping her head down. She attracted attention – the sort of attention Callum worked hard to avoid. He felt a bit sorry for her, but not enough to want to talk to her. With a half-hearted wave, he turned to head into the cafeteria.

'Hey, wait, Callum!'

Callum groaned inwardly. It didn't look like he had much choice now.

'You were there when Chloe was going on about those murders being done by a drug ring, weren't you?' Melissa asked, stopping halfway down the stairs as a boy pushed his way past her. 'What do you think?'

'I don't know,' Callum answered shortly. He didn't have time for Melissa's latest conspiracy theory. He was hungry, and the tips of his fingers were tingling annoyingly, as though his hands had fallen asleep.

'It's scary, though,' Melissa said.

'They're telling people not to panic.'

Melissa looked down at Callum and rolled her eyes. 'Of course that's what they tell you!'

The rush of kids finally stopped. There were just a few people still queuing for lunch, and now Melissa was the only person on the stairs. Except for that idiot Ed Bolton, crouched behind the railing at the top . . .

Callum looked up. From where he was standing, his view of the landing was obscured. What made him think Ed was there?

The tingling in his hands was worse now, real pins and needles, and suddenly he could see Ed quite

47

clearly, as if he was standing right next to him. The older boy *was* crouched behind the railing at the top of the stairs, with a squeezy dispenser of tomato sauce from the cafeteria. He was dripping ketchup in a steady stream over the railing, waiting for Melissa to walk beneath it.

Callum looked back at Melissa, but she was no longer standing on the stairs. She was stepping towards him . . . Stepping into a puddle of ketchup on one of the stairs. Slipping . . . Her foot sliding out from under her . . . Falling . . . Her head cracking against a concrete stair . . . Sliding . . . Until her body lay at the bottom of the stairwell in a limp tangle of silk, her head twisted at an unnatural angle, her eyes glassy and dead . . . And a dark pool of blood spreading out from her shattered skull . . . .

Then, as quickly as it had come, the tingling in his hands was gone.

Callum blinked, and there was Melissa, perfectly upright and unhurt, coming down the stairs. He shook his head. What he had seen hadn't been real. It couldn't have been.

But the red puddle at Melissa's feet *was*.

She was stepping towards it.

It was ketchup.

A blob of sauce hit Melissa on the cheek and she looked up, frowning, one foot hovering over the treacherous concrete step where the slippery pool waited.

Callum didn't hesitate. Leaping forward, he grabbed Melissa and yanked her towards him, so that she fell on to him instead of backwards on to the hard steps.

Melissa fell heavily, taking Callum down with her. They both collapsed in a heap at the bottom of the stairs in the sloppy mess of spilled tomato sauce. One of the boys in the lunch queue gave a whoop of delight.

'Roper and Scott! Woo-hoo!'

A couple of other boys laughed as Melissa untangled herself from Callum and wiped ketchup from her face, blinking and confused.

But she was alive. Callum closed his eyes. For a split-second he saw the vision again – Melissa lying on the stairs with her skull split wide open. When he

49

opened his eyes, the scene vanished.

Callum's head reeled. But it wasn't just the thought of what had almost taken place that sent his heart racing, it was what he had done.

He had seen it coming.

He had stopped it happening.

Chapter 6

'What the devil is going on here?'

It was Mr Gower, the deputy headmaster, his shining bald head red with outrage.

Melissa gave a wail as she realised she was covered with tomato sauce. She looked up to see where the drips were coming from and pointed. 'Someone's pouring ketchup down the stairs!'

'It's Ed Bolton,' Callum burst out, before the bully had a chance to flee the scene. No one could see him from down here, but Callum was so certain it was Ed that he didn't even think about the consequences of naming names.

'Bolton!' roared the deputy head. 'Get down here!'

Ed came skulking down the stairs. He gave Melissa a smirking, disdainful glance as he carefully skirted the mess of sauce on the steps, and shot Callum a meaningful look of warning. Finally he stood scowling before Mr Gower.

'This isn't a circus,' Mr Gower snapped over his shoulder at the gathering bunch of onlookers. 'Get to your class. Get to lunch. Get out of here. Not you, Scott, you seem to know it all. What happened here?'

Callum swallowed. Anything he said now would make a mortal enemy of Ed.

'I think it was an accident . . .' Callum began. Then, disgusted at his own cowardice, he straightened his shoulders. Ed was less frightening than the thing in the woods; Ed was something Callum knew how to fight, if he had to.

'No, I'm sorry, it wasn't,' Callum said boldly. 'Melissa was talking about vampires this morning, and Ed thought he'd tease her by dripping ketchup on her head. But I saw –'

Callum pulled himself up short. He couldn't tell

Mr Gower what he'd seen; he didn't even properly understand how he had seen it. And if he said anything about his vision of Melissa lying dead, they'd all think he was deranged.

'I saw that there was sauce on the stairs and Melissa was about to slip,' he continued. 'So I pulled her away from it, but we lost our balance and fell over.'

Mr Gower nodded. He glared at Ed.

'I've just about had it up to my eyeballs with your pranks, Bolton. Detention slips again, is it? But first, you've got a mess to clean up. Come to the caretaker's office and help yourself to a mop.' He pointed down the hall. 'Get on with it, Bolton.'

Ed threw Callum a look of pure hatred and marched off with the deputy head, leaving Callum and Melissa alone in the hall.

'Are you all right?' Callum asked awkwardly.

Melissa wiped her face with her spangled scarf.

'I'm OK. Thanks. Thanks for helping.'

'Do you need to get cleaned up?'

Melissa shook her head. 'This scarf only cost ninety pence at Shaman's – I'll just bin it. I'm going to lunch.

If I go up to the girls' toilets I'll have to pass Ed cleaning the floor on my way back down.'

Callum could see why Melissa might not want to risk that.

'All right.'

Callum followed Melissa into the cafeteria and they picked up their lunch trays without speaking. He was still shocked by what had happened. He had seen the future. He had *changed* the future.

There were two empty seats at the end of a table, so they sat down together.

'Cheer up,' Melissa said. 'At least you didn't get sauced.'

Callum couldn't help smiling.

'Ed's a bully,' he said. 'Don't take it personally. He's always looking for an excuse to make people look stupid.'

'Oh, I know. He's picked on me before. But not . . . not physically, you know?'

Callum realised suddenly that having their clothes ruined and being made to look stupid in front of half the school would have reduced a lot of other girls to tears. But Melissa just seemed resigned to it.

'Yeah, he picks on me too,' Callum told her sympathetically, poking at his mushy peas with his fork. 'Anyone who's not popular.'

'*You!*' said Melissa. 'What do you mean? Everybody likes you.'

Callum glanced up at her in surprise.

'Well, they do,' she said. 'You're good at sport. You don't talk much, but people *like* you. You're not a swot, you don't try to get in with the teachers, but you don't mess about either. Like today – you knew Ed was responsible and you weren't afraid to say so.'

Callum was astonished. Of course, you had to filter this news through Channel Melissa, but it had never occurred to him that popular kids like Hugh and Andrew spoke to him in the hall and helped him keep his eyes open in class because they liked him.

Melissa frowned a little, stabbing at her own plate. 'I hope he doesn't try and get back at you. How did you know it was him, anyway?'

'What d'you mean?'

'When you told Gower it was Ed dripping the ketchup, how did you know it was him?'

Callum bit his tongue.

'I just saw him, that's all.'

Melissa put down her fork.

'C'mon, you were standing in front of me, Callum. I was coming down the stairs, I could see the rail at the top, but I didn't notice Ed. You were standing at the *bottom* of the stairs, under the landing. You couldn't have seen him at all. How did you really know?'

'Must have been a lucky guess,' Callum countered evasively. He certainly wasn't going to tell her about his vision. 'You know Ed. If someone's dripping ketchup down the stairs, it's probably him.'

Melissa's brow furrowed, as if she was puzzling out something that didn't make sense.

'Yes, but when you pulled me out of the way, it was as though you knew something *terrible* was going to happen to me. Not like I was just going to get ketchup in my hair.'

'Look, anyone could see you might have slipped,' said Callum defensively. 'I didn't *know* anything.

56

How could I?' He stirred the green paste on his plate for emphasis.

'Yes, but –'

'Look, I've got to go,' said Callum abruptly, standing up and picking up his tray. He'd been here before – people noticing the strange things he could do. It always meant trouble. 'I'll see you later, OK.'

Callum didn't wait for a reply, but turned and headed out of the cafeteria. It wasn't just that Melissa's questions were getting a little too pointed. The truth was, even he didn't know the answers. It was more than luck; more even than his own special kind of Luck.

How *had* he known?

*

Ed was in both of his afternoon classes, so Callum spent the rest of the day slinking in and out of lessons at the last possible second, desperately trying to avoid an encounter. He had rugby practice after school, but luckily it lasted longer than Ed's detention, so the bully was long gone before he had finished. Still, he didn't want to chance it.

'Aren't you changing out of your kit?' asked Owen, the team captain, as Callum picked up his rucksack. 'You look like you've been mud wrestling.'

'I want to get home before dark,' Callum said.

'Can't say I blame you. Who'd want to walk through Marlock Wood at night!'

Though it wasn't exactly dark yet, the day was so overcast that twilight seemed to fall an hour earlier than usual. Marlock High Street was jammed with slow-moving traffic as commuters made their way home, and the shops were beginning to shut. The town's pavements were thick with the spirits of the dead.

Callum didn't think he'd ever seen so many ghosts in one place. Forgotten villagers from Marlock's thousand years of history lurked in doorways like gossiping smokers. Although he'd seen a few of them before, there seemed to be dozens of new ones – new to Callum, at least. As he waited to cross the road, the ghost of a wartime pilot, still in his smart blue uniform, stepped out in front of him. The spectral figure climbed up into an invisible bus and disappeared. A dead woman lay face down in the middle of the pavement, her long skirts flapping in a chill breeze only Callum seemed to feel. Another slumped against a post box, staring blankly at the sky and beckoning to someone invisible. It was like walking through a war zone that only he could see – normal passers-by hurried among the ghosts, oblivious to their presence.

Callum hunched his shoulders against the cold. Weren't ghosts supposed to haunt the places where they died? How could so many people have died in Marlock High Street? Or were they coming from somewhere else?

And how come, thought Callum bitterly as he reached the estate at the edge of town and turned on to the road that led down to Marlock Wood, *how come with all these ghosts, I don't just once see my own mum?*

'Hey, it's Scott! Look, it's Callum Scott! Been rolling in mud again, Scott?'

Ed and his gang were crouched under the wooden fort in the toddlers' play park at the edge of the estate, trying to keep their cigarettes out of the wind. Callum cursed himself. He'd been so distracted by the hordes of ghosts in town he'd forgotten that Ed lived around here.

He'd been lying in wait for him.

In a few seconds, the gang had Callum surrounded: Baz, Harry, George, Craig and Ed.

'Look at him, he must have been playing in a pigsty!'

That was Baz, Ed's best mate, always eager to please the boss.

'Nah, he just lives in one,' sneered Ed. 'Don't you, gyppo? You and your crazy gran.'

Callum gritted his teeth at the usual insult. 'Better than playing in a baby's sandpit,' he fired back.

He picked the biggest gap between Ed's buddies and set off at a fast walk. Maybe they wouldn't follow him into the woods. It was nearly dark now, and the ruined church didn't need a ghostly congregation to make it eerie.

But they did follow him. They kept up with him, walking as a group on his shoulder. Safety in numbers.

'You calling us babies, Scott?' Ed's voice dripped

with sarcasm. 'So why are you running away from a bunch of babies?'

Callum didn't reply.

'Hey! I asked you a question.'

'I didn't call you anything,' Callum said evasively.

'Yeah, but you shouted my name fast enough when you thought you could get Gower after me, didn't you?'

'Leave me alone,' Callum said, struggling to keep his voice level. They were well into the woods now, and the light was almost gone.

Someone laughed. 'He's running to tell his gran. Watch out, Ed – she'll turn you into a frog!'

'Frightened, Scott?' Ed gave him a shove that sent Callum stumbling forward. 'You should be.'

Callum clenched his fists, ground his teeth together and kept walking.

'Oi, Scott, you've got my hands dirty now.'

Callum spun around. 'Keep them to yourself, then!'

'Here, you can have your muck back,' said Ed, flicking his muddy hand towards Callum's face.

Callum reacted instinctively. He'd only really

intended to deflect Ed's blow, but instead his fist connected with the bully's leering face with a dull, wet crunch. An unexpected fountain of blood, almost black in the twilight, burst from Ed's nose. Ed staggered backwards into his mates. It took the gang a moment to reorganise. It took Callum a briefer moment to realise what he'd done.

God, how stupid!

He ran.

Callum could hear the noise of ten trainered feet pelting down the road only a few seconds behind him. There was no way he could outrun them. Through the trees, he saw the squat, black ruin of the old church tower, and instinctively swerved up the lane towards it. Maybe there would be somewhere to hide.

Nettles and brambles whipping at his shins, Callum dodged through the rusted iron gate. The churchyard was overgrown and filled with shadows. Callum was sure he'd be able to lose his pursuers among the worn tombstones.

He raced along the north side of the church, stumbling over graves. Stone angels stared down at him with blank eyes, their hands open in useless gestures of comfort. Where were the sword-wielding *guardian* angels when you needed them?

And where were the ghosts?

The sudden thought made Callum feel sick. Spectres had been crowding him off the pavement in Marlock High Street. Where the hell were they *now*? They were always here in the churchyard – except for today . . . and last night.

Callum veered round the north-east corner of the church and stopped dead. Standing no more than ten metres away, beneath the black and tossing branches of an ancient yew tree, was a boy. For an instant, Callum thought that one of Ed's gang had somehow cut him off. Then he looked closer, and his blood froze.

The boy seemed to be about Callum's age, but his melancholy eyes made him look older. He stood straight and alert. His clothes were old-fashioned – his long, high-necked jacket was so dark it seemed to blend into the falling night, while his deathly white face glowed with its own light. Mute at his side stood a dog the size of a lion, black as the inside of a well.

One of the boy's pale hands was buried in the shadow-fur of the beast's neck.

With chilling certainty, Callum knew that the pale figure wasn't a living human. And the strange familiarity between the boy and the dog made Callum sure that the creature wasn't mortal either. Its eyes glowed red, floating in the darkness of its head. Callum recognised their fiery gleam, and the waves of icy air that drifted from the beast towards him, tugging at his ankles. This monster was, without a doubt, the thing that had hunted him through the wood last night.

Neither the dog nor the boy moved. They were both staring at Callum. He took a shaking breath. No ghost had ever looked directly at him before. Callum had thought he was invisible to them, just as ghosts were invisible to most people. But these two – whatever they were – seemed to be able to see him.

'He went into the graveyard!'

Baz's voice broke the spell, jerking Callum back to himself. He glanced over his shoulder, but the church's low, solid bulk hid the path he had taken, so he couldn't tell how close his pursuers were.

Callum's mind raced. He had only two options – to try to go forwards, past the strange boy and his hell hound, or to fall back into the hands of Ed and his gang. He hesitated, his eyes flicking back to the dark pair. Slowly, the boy's bloodless mouth gave a twisted smile, as if mocking Callum's dilemma. The dog's lip curled upwards too, revealing a gleaming set of fangs.

Callum bolted. Turning on his heel, he tore back the way he had come, unable to bear the sight of the ghost-boy and his demon dog a moment longer. But before he had taken more than half a dozen steps, Ed and his gang came hurtling round the corner of the church, blocking his way.

Callum tried to gasp out a warning. 'Don't go on –'

'Don't worry,' Ed snarled. 'We're not going anywhere. And neither are you.'

As Ed stepped towards him, Callum saw the telltale gleam of a blade in the bully's right hand.

Then, behind Callum, the pale boy spoke a single, quiet word.

'Doom.'

And the dog at his side lifted up its head and howled.

THE SHADOWING

It was a noise beyond belief, like the shriek of steel on steel, thunderous and piercing – a sound so hideous that for one terrible second Ed literally cowered, riveted to the spot with his hands clapped over his ears. Then, as the howl slowly died away, he turned tail and fled. His gang followed him.

For a moment, Callum stood dumbstruck. Then he ran too.

Chapter 7

Callum didn't have any of the control he'd had last night. He didn't think logically about whether or not he should run from wild animals. He ran in blind terror. Out of the churchyard, down the lane, and on to the road home. With each jarring step, Callum imagined his ankles gripped from behind in those gleaming white fangs. Would the beast's breath feel hot against the back of his neck, or cold, like the icy wind that drifted around it? Could those bright, razor-sharp fangs tear human flesh, or did they sink into your heart and freeze you to death without even drawing blood? Callum drew another ragged breath and drove himself faster.

He tripped and fell, tearing open both knees and both palms, but he scrambled to his feet again and ran on, skidding in the fallen leaves that gathered in piles along the road. He never looked behind him, expecting any second to feel the black monster leap on to his back.

The lit window of the lonely cottage beckoned, and Callum sprinted towards it. Hurdling the low garden wall, he caught his anorak on one of Gran's rose bushes, and had to rip it free. With a final effort, he threw himself inside and slammed the door behind him.

He closed his eyes and leaned against the door, panting and gasping as he slid to the floor.

'What in the world?!'

Callum opened his eyes as Gran raced out of the kitchen. In his mind's eye, he saw what she saw – her teenage grandson collapsed on the doorstep, covered with mud and dead leaves, his knees and hands bloody, his hair probably standing on end. It was the second night in a row he'd come bursting into the cottage with his teeth chattering.

'What happened?' Gran demanded.

'I got chased by that dog,' Callum gasped, not stopping to think about what he should say.

'What, again? Was it one of Warren's? A farmer ought to be able to keep his dogs under control!'

'No, Gran,' Callum interrupted, still panting. 'It wasn't a farm dog. Warren's got Border collies. This one was completely black, no white anywhere, and it was –'

He stopped himself blurting out, *It was as big as a horse*. He didn't want to sound like an idiot. Or a baby.

'It was much bigger than a sheepdog.' A horrible thought struck him. 'Gran, Cadbury's not outside, is he?'

'He was asleep in your laundry basket, last time I looked.' Gran strode to the front window and pressed her face to the leaded glass. 'Where did you see it?'

'The cat?' Callum asked in confusion.

'The *dog*, of course,' Gran said sharply. 'Where did it come from? How far did it chase you?'

'From the church,' Callum replied, although actually, now his mind wasn't paralysed with terror, he realised that he wasn't absolutely sure it *had* chased him. He had been too terrified to look back. Surely a creature that size could have caught him easily, if it had tried. And if it hadn't chased him, was that because it was busy with Ed and his mates? What was going on in the churchyard *now*?

'A big dog? Size of a Shetland pony? Completely black, from nose to tail?'

'Yeah, except for its teeth!' Callum peeled leaves away from his shins and glanced up at Gran suspiciously. Her Sherlock Holmes-type questions were out of character. He had expected her to dismiss the whole thing as fear of the dark and then start fussing over his skinned knees, but she was still staring keenly out of the window. Her next question was even more unexpected.

'Was there a boy with it?'

Callum's breath caught in his throat. How could Gran possibly know about the boy? When he didn't reply, Gran spun around and repeated the question more forcefully.

'Did you see its owner too?'

'Why does it matter?' Callum demanded. 'I was chased by a dog, not a person!'

'It's the owner who's responsible,' Gran answered.

'But what makes you think the owner is a boy?'

Something wasn't right. Callum could tell that Gran was holding back. Did she know something about what was going on? That morning she'd seemed overly worried about him walking home in the dark, now she was asking these unsettlingly precise questions. It was like she was fishing for information but not wanting to give anything away herself.

'Have you seen it?' he pressed. 'This black dog. Do you know who owns it?'

'No, Callum, I haven't seen it.'

Gran stared into his eyes for a long moment. Callum met her gaze steadily. He wanted to tell her that there *had* been a boy with the dog, but why should he, if she wasn't being open with him? Finally, Gran sighed. 'Well, I'll have a word with Warren tomorrow. Maybe he's got a new dog. Why don't you go and get yourself cleaned up. Fish pie tonight.'

That was that. Gran crossed the room and went

back out to the kitchen. It was about as close to a brush-off as she was capable of. She hadn't even bothered to complain about the mud he'd tracked across the sitting room.

Frustrated, frightened and rattled, Callum tidied up the mess and unpacked his rucksack. He and his grandmother didn't talk much over supper, but she didn't seem angry. Callum glanced up from beneath his tangled hair, still wet after his bath. Gran was staring at the fire as she ate, her look distant.

Callum spread his homework over the table while Gran washed up. She didn't turn on the radio like she usually did. Callum found himself wondering if she was avoiding another ugly news report. Whatever the reason, Gran's strange behaviour made him even more convinced that something was definitely wrong.

*

That night, he lay awake for what seemed like hours again. The rowan tree scratched at the window and the frame rattled as usual. Callum strained his ears, listening for howling. He was going to be a mess by the end of the week if he didn't get more sleep. And then there was Ed to face again tomorrow, assuming he hadn't been eaten alive. Ed, who'd pulled a knife on him. Callum took a long, deep breath. It was bad enough he had ghosts trying to kill him, without his classmates joining in . . .

'I wish I knew what was going on, Cad,' murmured Callum. Cadbury was unresponsive, a sleeping heap of fur in his favourite spot at Callum's feet. The cat gave a little sigh when he heard Callum's voice, but didn't raise his head.

Callum stared up at the low ceiling. He could hear Gran still pottering about downstairs. Was she getting the table out again? Maybe she was setting up her easel. Whatever she was doing, the sound of her dragging furniture around wasn't helping him get to sleep.

'OK,' he said finally. 'A hot drink, that's what I need.'

His mum always used to make him hot milk when he couldn't sleep. If he got it quietly himself, maybe Gran wouldn't make a fuss.

Callum slipped out of his bed. God, it was *freezing*.

He reached for a jumper and shrugged it on over his pyjamas before heading to the door. He didn't bother to switch on the light – the stairs were dimly illuminated by the glow coming up from the sitting room. He made his way slowly down the small spiral staircase, hugging the wall where the steps were widest, feeling the way with his bare feet on the uneven treads.

As he turned the corner at the bottom of the spiral, Callum opened his mouth to speak, but stopped. Gran was standing on a chair by the window, her back to him, busy with something on the highest of the bookshelves – the one that ran above the window and the door. You couldn't even see that shelf unless you stood practically beneath it, because one of the ancient timber beams holding up the ceiling ran in front of it. What was she doing?

Quietly, Callum took another step down the stairs.

As he watched, Gran pulled down several books, stacking them carefully on the edge of one of the lower shelves. Callum stared, intrigued. What were the books? Gardening or painting manuals by the look of it; there were flowers and jugs and landscapes on the covers. Callum didn't pay much attention to the books Gran kept on the inaccessible shelves – they were mostly ones that even *she* never bothered to read. Maybe she'd decided to get rid of them. But it seemed a very strange time of day for a clear-out.

Gran stopped her work suddenly. She stood with her hands on her hips, scanning the shelf in front of her. After a moment she reached back – far back – and pulled out another book. Callum realised that the shelf was deeper than he had first thought. The book Gran had pulled out had been behind the books at the front of the shelf.

Gran blew a layer of dust off the top edge of the book and examined the spine. It was bound in black leather and stitched with silver; the fine detail glimmered in the firelight as she opened the cover and studied the first page. Finally, she set this book aside, wiped her dusty hands on the back of her trousers and put back all the other books in their original places. Then she climbed down from her chair.

Callum quietly retreated a couple of steps into the shadows. He listened while she moved the chair back into its place under the table. Silence fell. After a minute or two, Callum dared to steal a glance round the stair wall.

Gran was sitting in her armchair by the fire with the decaying black and silver book open in her lap. The reflection of the fire's orange flames danced in her reading glasses. She was so absorbed she did not look up.

What on Earth was she doing?

For long minutes, Callum waited, growing steadily colder as he watched for any clue as to what his grandmother was reading, but she gave no sign. Finally, with a deep sigh, she closed the cover. Callum ducked back into the shadows. His teeth were chattering, but his blood burned with frustrated curiosity. What was that book? And why had Gran been hiding it? There was no way of knowing – it wasn't as if he could just pop down and ask her, and it was too cold to hang around hoping she would give something away. Reluctantly, Callum turned to make his way quietly back to bed. With every step up the narrow staircase, the draught danced around his feet, like icy fangs snapping at his heels.

Chapter 8

Callum barely made it to his first class on time. He had spent so long skulking in the back streets of Marlock trying to avoid Ed and his mates that he had to duck into his English lesson without even taking off his coat and rucksack. He dodged out of class the instant the bell rang and raced to his locker. But his plan backfired. Mrs Higgins stopped him to give him a telling-off for running, and Ed slouched past slowly, enjoying the spectacle. He caught Callum's eye and mouthed, *'You're dead'*.

Ed had disappeared by the time Mrs Higgins was finished with Callum, but he was late for his next class as well and was in more trouble for that.

The talk in the cafeteria at lunch was still all about yesterday's murdered teen. One of the tabloids had managed to sneak a photographer into the alley where the body was discovered, and now the bloody message Callum had seen scrawled on the wall in his dream was plastered all over the front page. The accompanying article was as stuffed with unanswered questions as Callum's own head.

Although it seemed like he had seen ghosts every day of his life, Callum knew almost nothing about the supernatural. Now that he felt he needed to know more, he didn't know where to begin. He'd never read a ghost story, or watched a horror film. Who needed stories about ghosts when you saw real ones on every corner?

I bet Melissa Roper reads ghost stories, though, Callum thought. She was into alternative stuff like healing crystals and dreamcatchers, and she was always clutching the latest fantasy novel. Maybe she could help him.

As if on cue, he spotted her, sitting on her own as

usual, on the far side of the room. Well, there was no time like the present . . .

Melissa looked up in surprise as Callum set down his lunch tray next to her.

'Hey, Callum!'

'Hi,' Callum replied sheepishly. 'Do you mind if I sit here?'

'Go ahead,' smiled Melissa. Callum sat. 'Thanks again for yesterday, by the way. Guess it got you in trouble with Ed Bolton, though.'

'You've no idea.' Callum forced a laugh. There wasn't any point in dragging Melissa into *that* mess. 'Listen, I wanted to ask you something . . . You know about the supernatural, right?'

'Well, I know some stuff,' Melissa answered eagerly. 'You know, like traditional charms, how to protect your cows from curses and your babies from being kidnapped by goblins. Stuff like that.'

Callum must have looked blank, because Melissa rolled her eyes and went on.

'Everybody knows about how vampires hate garlic, right? Well, there are charms like that for all kinds of things. Iron keeps away the fairies. Rowan works against witches and demons.'

'Really?' It had never occurred to Callum that he might be able treat ghosts like a medical condition – take two rowan berries and get rid of your haunting, like taking paracetamol for a headache. 'That's pretty interesting.'

'It *is* interesting,' said Melissa, nodding furiously. Then she stopped. 'You're not taking the mickey, are you?'

'No, no, I mean it,' said Callum quickly. Melissa probably had every reason to be defensive. She got teased a lot – even if she did bring some of it on herself. 'How about *local* legends?' he added tentatively. 'Do you know any local ghosts?'

'Well, not personally,' Melissa laughed. 'I haven't met any. There's a haunted cinema in Altrincham where the projectors turn themselves on and off, and the seats are always snapping up and down. I've been there,' she added proudly. 'And at Knutsford there's a ghost pig that runs around the lanes with six lighted candles on its back. Every place has local ghosts.

Some of them mean special things. If you see a banshee washing clothes in a river, that means you're going to die.'

Callum looked sideways at Melissa. 'How about black dogs? What does it mean if you see the ghost of a black dog?'

'They mean a lot of things.' Melissa frowned and blew her flyaway curly fringe out of her eyes. 'There are black dogs in folklore all over Britain. They've got about a million different names – Black Shuck, Striker, Trash. Also Wist Wolves and Yell Hounds, Churchyard Grims –'

'Wait!' Callum exclaimed, holding up a hand to stop Melissa mid-flow. 'Churchyard Grims. Tell me about those.'

'The Grim is a portent of death.' Melissa's eyes went very wide. 'They're big, black dogs that haunt burial grounds. They're supposed to be the ghosts of animals that have been sacrificed to the devil – the devil takes take the animal's soul in place of the human souls buried there, you see. Or else the Grim is supposed to protect the human souls buried there from the devil. I forget which. Maybe both.'

Callum's mind raced. There was a name for the black dog he'd seen. It was a Churchyard Grim. He hadn't made it up. It was a portent of death, a sacrifice to hell. No wonder Gran had been spooked when Callum asked about a black dog.

But since when did Gran know anything about the supernatural? She was practical and down-to-earth, with her gardening books and her DIY battles with the immersion heater. So why had she reacted so strangely? It didn't make sense.

'Is that helpful?' Melissa prompted. Callum jumped out of his reverie and realised he'd been staring straight at her during the lull in the conversation. He looked away quickly, and fixed his gaze on his chips.

'Yeah, thanks.'

'Why did you want to know anyway?'

'I live near an old churchyard,' Callum said. 'You know, Nether Marlock. I just wondered if it had any stories connected with it.'

Melissa gave him a sharp look. 'Black dogs especially?'

Callum sighed. 'Yeah.'

83

'Have you *seen* it?' Melissa asked softly.

Callum put his elbows on the table and his head in his hands, pulling at his hair. He couldn't decide what to tell her. He didn't know her very well, after all, and the truth would make him sound like a crazy freak.

'You've seen something, haven't you?' Melissa's voice was eager. She didn't sound like she thought he was crazy; she just sounded curious. 'What was it?'

'I don't know.'

'If I came along home with you after school sometime you could show me where you saw it. I love that old church. All those medieval gravestones with the skulls on them, and that yew tree that's supposed to be a thousand years old! I could come and take a look, see if I know what it is, the thing you saw – if we see it again, I mean.'

'I don't know,' Callum repeated reluctantly. 'Maybe I was just imagining it.'

'Maybe you weren't,' said Melissa. 'And maybe I can help.'

Callum let out a long breath. It had taken Melissa less than ten minutes to prove that she knew more about the supernatural than he ever would.

He smiled at her again.

'Maybe you can.'

*

There was a double period of science after lunch, a lab class on Elements and Compounds. Callum liked the chemistry teacher, who made a real effort to keep her students interested, but in spite of Dr MacKenzie's best efforts, Callum was having trouble focusing. His mind was still in Marlock Wood.

Dr MacKenzie was exploding bubbles. She had spread a mess of apparently harmless froth on the fireproof lab table and was setting the bubbles alight with a gas jet pipe attached to a Bunsen burner. Each bubble she lit made a sudden, loud explosion of orange flame.

'Melissa, come and have a go.'

'You must be joking,' called Ed Bolton from the back of the class. 'She'll burn the whole school down.'

The class laughed and Melissa flushed.

'Come on, Melissa, it's perfectly safe.' Dr MacKenzie handed over the gas jet. Melissa took it tentatively.

'OK, now just touch one of the bubbles with the flame.'

Melissa stretched out her arm, holding the flame as far from her body as possible, and went for the smallest of the bubbles. The gas compound inside it exploded with a little burst of fire, and was gone. Ed cheered sarcastically.

'Callum?'

Callum jumped. He hadn't been paying attention. He looked up guiltily.

'You're missing a great effect. Have a go.'

Dr MacKenzie walked around the table towards him.

'No thanks, Dr MacKenzie,' Callum said. 'I'll do it wrong.'

'Nonsense. There's nothing to it. When you've seen how the experiment works, we'll run through the formula again.'

'Have a go, Scott, show Roper the right way to do it,' said Hugh Mayes.

Callum sighed inwardly. He'd have to do it now.

He reached for the flaming pipe, his fingertips feeling numb. He shook his hand, trying to wake them up, but the tingling was getting worse. Tingling . . .

MOVE!

Without stopping to question the urge, Callum leaped sideways, almost falling into the lap of the girl in the next seat. At the same instant, Dr MacKenzie caught her foot on a large bookbag carelessly left jutting out from under the table. Grabbing at the ledge of the worktop to catch her balance, the flame-tipped hosepipe flew from her hand. Spewing its jet of burning gas, the pipe landed in the chair where Callum had been sitting less than a second earlier. Before Dr MacKenzie could straighten herself up and turn off the gas tap, the blue flame had burnt a sizeable hole into the back of Callum's chair.

If he had still been sitting there, the flame would have bored the same hole straight through his chest.

Chaos erupted in the classroom. Several of the girls screamed.

'Callum! Are you OK?' Dr MacKenzie gasped. 'My God, how did you ever get out of the way in time?'

For a moment Callum was speechless. Finally he managed to murmur numbly, 'I . . . I saw you lose your balance. I just moved.'

'Thank goodness! I'm so sorry. Katie, how many times have I told you not to bring that bag into my classroom . . .'

The teacher's voice faded away as Callum tuned out her angry words. His mind was already miles away. Because he knew full well that he hadn't seen her lose her balance. He'd been moving *before* she had tripped, without any idea why he was doing it.

His Luck had saved him again.

*

What's happening to me?

The visions, his tingling fingertips, the strange hauntings – and if all this weren't enough, there was Ed to deal with too. After the final bell went, Callum was out of the school building ahead of almost everybody, but not Ed. He was already heading down the high street with Baz and Craig, no doubt planning to lie in wait for Callum again.

Callum stood still and watched them go; there was no point in hurrying now. Better to take the scenic route, down Back Lane and along the footpath through the fields behind Warren's farm. Ed and his foot-soldiers would never think of going all the way out there.

The other advantage of the long walk was that the last stretch along the lower edge of Marlock Wood avoided the church. He still had to pass the shell of the old mill, with its two spectral mutilated young apprentices who'd had the bad luck to fall under the waterwheel, but there weren't as many ghosts as on the road.

It was dusk when Callum finally trudged along the row of ruined alms cottages, their broken windows dark and their empty rooms open to the sky. For a moment, he was surprised to see that there was no light beckoning from the window of Gran's cottage. Then he remembered – it was Thursday, the evening she taught a watercolour class in the church hall up in the town. He was supposed to get tea ready for them both. Cheese toasties again, probably.

As he reached down to unhook the gate, Callum realised that this was the first time in three days that he'd actually bothered to go through the gate rather than jumping over the wall in blind terror. Letting out a short, mirthless laugh, Callum walked up the garden path towards the front door, reaching for his key.

And stopped.

Something had happened to the door. Dark splatters stained its green paint. They looked almost wet, but it hadn't been raining. Besides, the shapes reminded him of something . . .

As Callum took a step back for a clearer view, the shapes came into focus and his stomach plummeted into his trainers.

It was a message written in blood.

There was just enough light in the sky for him to make out the glistening letters, shining black against the faded green paint. Although some of the writing had run, the letters dripping dark, clotting tails down the door, the ghastly message was still clear enough to read.

BEWARE THE DARK REFLECTION

Callum stared at the words. He had no doubt the message was for him – and written by the same person as the writing found beside the murdered boy in London. Whoever they were, they had found him.

Fear rising, Callum fumbled in his pocket for the key. His fingers were trembling. No, not trembling – *tingling* . . .

Callum whirled round.

Standing at the gate, less than a dozen paces away, were the ghostly white-faced boy and his demonic black dog.

The Grim's teeth flashed in its pitch-black muzzle. Callum took one terrified step backwards down the garden path, then another, waiting for the creature to pounce.

But the strange dog remained still, a low growl rumbling in its throat. Instead, its pale master began to walk slowly towards Callum, his right hand held out as if to touch him, and in the last of the fading daylight, Callum saw that the boy's thin, white fingers were dripping with glistening blood.

Chapter 9

His hand clutched tightly around the cold metal key in his pocket, Callum took another slow step backwards.

Don't run! Don't run!

Another step. Callum swallowed, preparing himself. His only chance was to get into the cottage. To put ten centimetres of solid door between him and this terror. The dead boy was at the open gate, still walking steadily towards him, his depthless eyes fixed on Callum.

Beware the dark reflection . . .

Was that what the message was warning against – the dark reflection of this boy's eyes? Another step. How many more before he reached the cottage? The boy was on the path now, the huge dog prowling at his heel. Callum didn't imagine that the door would hold the Grim for long.

They were too close. He wasn't going to make it . . .

Callum felt his heel bump against the doorstep. Moving like lightning, he half-twisted around, slamming his body against the door as he twisted the key in the lock.

For once, the latch turned first time.

The door flew open under the force of Callum's impact. Caught off balance, he fell over the threshold and tumbled into the dark sitting room. He scrambled backwards, trying to kick the door shut, but the hem of his anorak, ragged where he'd torn it on the rose bush the previous night, caught beneath the door and jammed it open.

Nearly crying with terror and frustration, Callum tried to tear his coat loose. With sheer brute force he ripped it out from under the door. He was free now, but with the torn part of his anorak bunched up against the carpet, the door still wouldn't shut.

The figure of the pale boy seemed to fill the

doorway. One more step and he'd be in the house, and Callum would be alone in the darkness with him and the black dog . . .

'STOP!' Callum yelled desperately, his voice cracking with fear. 'STAY OUT!'

The spectral boy flinched as if Callum had struck him. He actually took a step backwards and teetered on the edge of the doorstep.

For half a second, Callum was too surprised to move. Then, pulling himself up on to his knees on the worn carpet, he cried out wildly, 'GET AWAY! STAY OUT OF THIS HOUSE! YOU CAN'T COME IN!'

The phantom stumbled. He was off the doorstep now. He lifted one foot to try to bring it forwards, but it was as if an unseen hand was preventing it. His eyes flashed with anger. Beside him, the black dog gave a chilling growl of frustration.

Callum took a deep breath and tried to get a grip.

'Just. Stay. Out.' Callum glared at the spirit as fiercely as he could as he tugged at the shredded nylon wedging the door open.

Astonishingly – unbelievably – the ghost answered.

'I can't come in.'

Callum froze. The ghost was talking to him. The boy's voice was hollow and echoing, as though he was speaking from the bottom of a well. Just the sound of it was enough to raise goosebumps on Callum's exposed arms.

'What's stopping you?' Callum demanded.

'You are.'

Callum straightened up slowly. His heart was still thundering in his ears. Surely it couldn't be that simple. Was he really safe, or was the ghost-boy playing some trick?

'What about your dog?' he said. He could see the enormous beast behind its master, crouching on the brick path like a great black shadow.

'Doom cannot enter either.' The pale boy shrugged. 'Few creatures of the Netherworld can cross your threshold unless invited. And certainly not if you have expressly forbidden it.'

The spectre waved a hand at the tree overhead. 'Rowan at the door, and holly growing under all the windows. They, too, are barriers.' The boy's bell-like voice was compelling. Callum found himself paying close attention to each word.

'I hardly dare venture one step off this path into your grandmother's garden, for her beds and borders are rife with such old wards,' the boy continued. 'Ash, hazel, garlic . . .' The boy gave a twisted smile, revealing sharp, white teeth. 'She keeps you well guarded.'

'Garlic?' Callum tensed. 'Are you some sort of vampire?'

'Nothing so mundane. My name is Jacob.'

Even in the dark, Callum could see cold amusement on the ghost's face. It glowed with a pale light of its own, faint, but enough to illuminate the bloody letters on the door.

'Did you write that?'

The ghost gave a single nod.

'Whose blood is it?' Callum asked.

'Mine,' replied Jacob, holding up his emaciated right hand. Liquid trickled down the slender fingers, crimson against the bone-white skin. 'As was the blood I used in my last warning. You are in danger. Mortal danger.'

Callum leaped to his feet.

'Don't threaten me!' he shouted, flicking the switch for the outside light. Callum thought that ghosts were supposed to prefer the dark, but the electric lamp had no effect on the spectre at the door. If anything, the contrast made his black hair darker, his eyes more depthless. The dog behind him was hidden in shadow.

'You are being hunted,' said Jacob, narrowing his eyes. 'Surely you have seen it – boys and girls like you, murdered.'

Callum flinched at the brutal words, his mind flying back to the alley in his dream. The broken body of the boy, his eyes torn out. The idea that he might have some sort of connection to the mutilated corpses found across the country made him feel sick, as though *he* were somehow responsible for the killings, instead of this *thing* on his doorstep.

'Listen,' snarled Callum, renewing his efforts to free the door. 'You may have killed those others, but I'm different. I can *see* you.'

The ghost's expression did not change.

'The others could see me too. But they did not heed my warnings. Now they are dead.'

'I'm not afraid of you,' said Callum, finally tugging the door loose.

The ghost boy saw what was coming. He reached out to prevent Callum from closing the door, but he couldn't even put his gleaming hands over the doorstep. Whether it was Gran's rowan tree or Callum's command, something was holding him back.

'You can't hide what you are,' hissed the ghost furiously. 'You can't change it. You must fight. Or you will die like the others.'

'Well I'm not like them,' Callum said furiously.

'But you are,' retorted Jacob. 'You are just like them – only stronger. This is your destiny. One of you must fight back if you want to save the others.'

'What others? It's nothing to do with me!'

'The others like you,' replied the ghost. 'All those born between the chimes. The dead ones were all born in the chime hours.'

Callum shook his head, confusion raging in his mind.

'I don't have any idea what you're talking about!'

For the first time, a flicker of doubt passed over the white face.

'Can it be? Can you truly not know the truth about our kind?'

'Our kind? What do you think I am?' Callum cried in frustration.

Jacob gave a smile that almost froze his blood.

'You are a chime child. Like me.'

Callum slammed the door.

Chapter 10

It has come a long way. Distance and effort mean nothing to the Hunter; time does not age it. But the time between kills makes it hungry. It understands time.

Instinct has brought it to a place of tangled trees. It can sense the leaf mould of long centuries at rest here. This has never been a place for flesh and blood to live, though at the old wood's heart is one of their flimsy sacred piles of stone, and down where the wood thins stands a row of ruined, empty dwellings.

The next human victim is close. The Hunter can sense its presence. Hunger draws them together. But the Hunter cannot tell precisely where its target waits.

It pauses in the wood, straining to follow the tantalising glimmer of the victim's energy, that power that makes this one worth the chase. The Hunter's hunger grows piercing.

Then, suddenly, as though a door has been slammed, the energy is gone.

There is nothing. No clue, no guide.

This has never happened before.

The Hunter is furious. It is happy to be challenged, but it will not be mocked.

With lithe, supernatural stealth, it moves swiftly through the trees. It cannot sense its victim any more, but it remembers the row of ruined dwelling places.

Perhaps not all of them are empty.

The Hunter must feed.

Chapter 11

Callum leaned against the door, breathing hard. His heart was beating wildly. After a moment, he threw the bolt across and double-locked the door. Then he ran through the cottage, pulling all the curtains closed, determined to shut out the horrors beyond them.

Back in the sitting room, he looked around. The jar of rowan berries and hazel leaves still stood on the table. Melissa had told him about their powers of protection against the supernatural – now he had seen it at first hand. Was it just a coincidence that the cottage was filled with them?

Yes, of course it was. Gran was an artist. The leaves

and berries were pretty. She was probably planning to use them in one of her paintings.

Still, even surrounded by their protective power, Callum wished he wasn't going to be in the house alone for the next hour and a half. What were you supposed to do when a demonic spectre defaces your door with his own dripping blood? Dial 999? Yeah, right . . .

Two bloody messages in two days, Callum thought, shuddering. He had tried to convince himself that the first one wasn't meant for him, even though he couldn't see any possible way he could have known about it before the news was made public. But the message on the door – there could be no denying who that was intended for. Was Jacob telling the truth when he claimed they were warnings? And what did they have to do with Callum being a . . . what had the boy called him?

A chime child.

'Born in the chime hours . . .' Callum murmured. That didn't make any sense either. How could the time he was born make a difference?

And all the other murder victims – even if they had been born at the same time, why would that make someone want to kill them all?

Callum stormed around the little cottage trying to convince himself that everything was normal. Table, pulled out. Jar of rowan (pretty berries, no more than that), on the mantelpiece. Homework, on the table. Kettle, on the gas ring –

The front door shook. Someone was rapping smartly on the round brass knocker.

Callum froze. Had the ghostly boy been standing out there all this time, waiting? Did he think Callum was likely to respond to a polite knock by opening the door again and inviting him in?

'Go away!' he shouted.

'Oh, I'm sorry,' replied a muffled voice from the other side of the door. It was a girl's voice, a human voice. It sounded apologetic and surprised, and other than that, normal.

Callum stepped closer to the door. After a moment's hesitation he demanded, 'Who's there?'

'It's Melissa. Melissa Roper, you know, from school?'

Callum's heart sank. If it *was* Melissa, he couldn't leave her standing there on the same side of the door where Jacob and his demonic dog were lurking. But what if it wasn't Melissa? What if it was a trick? Callum bit his lip.

'What do you want?' The question came out more rudely than he'd intended. But he hoped her answer might give him a clue about whether it really was Melissa.

'I didn't mean to disturb you. I've brought you my . . .'

Melissa's voice carried on, even more muffled than before, so Callum couldn't make out what it was saying. Carefully, he undid the lock and the bolt and opened the door a crack, wedging his body behind it so he could slam it shut if he had to. He peered through the gap.

It was Melissa all right, standing beneath the porch light. She'd changed out of her school clothes and wore a long velvet skirt and a leaf-green cape. Over her shoulder was an obviously heavy bag decorated with tiny mirrors.

'You've brought me your Pictish Fiction of the Actual?' he said dubiously.

Melissa laughed. For all her airy-fairy gear she looked solidly alive and normal. *'British Dictionary of the Supernatural,'* she said. 'It's got your black dog in it. I thought you might like to have a look. And I said I'd help.'

'How'd you know where to find me?'

'Everybody knows where you live, Callum.'

Callum was not reassured. Melissa laughed again. 'Your gran's address is in the post office window, you know. Pet portraits and watercolours for sale. Can I come in, or do you really want me to go away?'

Callum scanned the garden behind her, but could see no sign of Jacob or Doom. He opened the door a bit wider so Melissa wouldn't think he was a paranoid lunatic, and Cadbury came streaking into the house, his tail bristling like a toilet brush. Melissa giggled, and Callum felt himself relax slightly.

'No – no. You can come in,' said Callum, glad to have human company. He pulled the door fully open. 'Sorry about the graffiti.'

'Graffiti?' Melissa replied.

Callum looked down at the door's faded green paint. The dripping, bloody letters were gone.

'Nothing. Forget it.'

Callum chewed his bottom lip. Maybe ghost blood was as insubstantial as a ghost itself.

Melissa stepped easily over the threshold, frowning a little. As she put her bag down on the floor with a thump, it fell open, revealing a bundle of books. She straightened up, stretching, and looked around the room as Callum shut the door behind her and double locked it.

'Wow,' Melissa said. 'Bringing you a bag full of books is sort of like carrying coals to Newcastle, isn't it!'

'They're Gran's,' said Callum.

'What, haven't you read *any* of them?'

'Gran's taste is pretty dire,' Callum answered. 'Modern romance and nineteenth-century novels. And gardening and painting.'

'Bet you'd find something if you looked.'

'D'you want a hot chocolate?' Callum asked. 'I was just getting ready to do my homework.'

'I'm sorry. You don't like being interrupted, do you?' Melissa said. 'You sounded pretty angry when you answered the door. I could come back another time.'

'No, it's fine. To tell you the truth –'

Callum stopped himself. He *couldn't* tell her the truth.

Instead he told her something close to the truth, something believable. 'I thought you were Ed Bolton. He's been out for revenge since that run-in with Gower yesterday. Look, let me get the fire going and boil the kettle, and I'll take a look at your book.'

'You do the fire, I'll make the hot chocolate,' said Melissa.

'OK.'

Callum stirred up the embers as Melissa headed into the kitchen. She was quick but very messy. She managed to get milk all over the worktop, which Cadbury gladly attempted to clean up, and left rings of chocolate everywhere. But she was finished in no time.

'So,' she said, thumping herself down on the hearthrug with two steaming mugs, the breeze of her skirts stirring the flames in the grate. 'Wow, cosy. I love this place. OK. Look, this is my *Dictionary of the*

Supernatural. Here's the entry on the Churchyard Grim.'

Callum sat down beside her while Melissa read aloud.

'"A Churchyard Grim is the spirit of a dog buried alive in a graveyard to act as a guardian for those laid to rest there."' She paused and made a face. 'Ew, I'd forgotten about the buried alive bit. So in theory it's not really dead, I guess – an immortal dog. But a *good* dog, since it's supposed to be protecting people!'

'Who'd expect loyalty and protection from something they'd buried alive?' Callum replied, half laughing and half appalled.

'Dunno,' Melissa said, and took a gulp of hot chocolate, liberally sprinkling her long skirt with drips as she put the mug back on the hearth. 'I don't think the people who buried dogs in graveyards were very logical. It says that in Wales they used pigs instead of dogs!'

'You're really making a mess,' Callum said as Melissa slopped yet more chocolate on herself.

'I know. I can't help it. Pretend it's holy water – protection against evil spirits.' Melissa shook her flyaway curly hair back out of her face and turned the page of the book. '"A Grim loves the sound of church bells and can be pacified by their ringing." Look, there's a picture.'

Callum peered over her shoulder. The illustration showed a seventeenth-century engraving of a shaggy black beast as big as a bear. The size was about right, he reckoned, but it didn't look much like a dog. Callum shivered. The creature from the woods hadn't looked much like a dog either when he'd first seen it. But at least the book proved that the monster wasn't just a product of his own imagination. Maybe it could be helpful in other areas . . .

'Hey,' Callum said. 'Does this book say anything about chime children?'

'Chime children?'

'Yeah. Does it say what a chime child is?'

Melissa picked up the book and propped it against her knees as she found the entry and began to read out loud.

'"Chime child. Born beneath the light of a full moon in the 'chime hours' between midnight on Friday and cockcrow on Saturday. Until the age of eighteen, a chime child is gifted with unnatural luck, an uncanny ability to foresee future events, and the power to see ghosts. A chime child may also be able to sense the presence of evil spirits or of living beings of evil intent."' Melissa paused. 'Wow, that could be helpful.'

'Helpful!' Callum echoed in disbelief. 'Seeing ghosts could be helpful?'

'No, knowing the future. Knowing about evil intent. Like guessing Ed Bolton's plans for you –'

Melissa looked up at Callum suddenly, her eyes wide. 'That's how you knew!'

Callum shook his head. 'Knew what?'

'Knew that Ed was up there at the top of the stairs yesterday, even though you couldn't see him. You knew something was going to happen to me, and you stopped it happening.'

'I –'

Melissa wouldn't let him interrupt. 'And again today in science. You knew something was going to happen there, too! You jumped out of your chair for no reason, and you didn't get hurt!'

Melissa slapped the book face down on the hearth.

111

Her mug wobbled, cocoa splashing down the sides. Callum grabbed it before it could fall over.

'It doesn't mean anything,' he protested. 'I was lucky.'

'*Unnaturally* lucky! Premonitions of the future, unnaturally lucky, and you can see ghosts, can't you? That's why you asked about the Church Grims. You've seen one, haven't you?'

Callum shook his head, his lips pressed together. He couldn't answer. All his life he'd avoided talking about his strange abilities, as if keeping silent about them made them less real. But now that didn't seem to be working any more. His abilities were pushing their way into his life, whether he liked it or not.

'Say no if the answer's no!' Melissa commanded, her big eyes wide. Callum stared back at her, trying to gauge her mood. She wasn't angry and she wasn't sceptical. She was . . . well, the only word for it was *excited*. She thought this was an adventure. Maybe even fun.

Callum looked away. It didn't feel fun or exciting to him.

'Go on – say no! Tell me you can't see ghosts!'

'I can,' Callum said fiercely. 'All right? I can. I see ghosts *everywhere*.'

It was an embarrassment and a huge relief, all at the same time, to say it aloud to another person – to a human, not a bird or a cat. Or a ghost.

'Wow,' Melissa breathed, and fell silent.

Callum couldn't bring himself to say anything more. He stared at the fire, sipping at his own mug of hot chocolate, his knees drawn up close to his chest.

After a moment, Melissa stirred.

'Can you see them here? Now?' she asked softly.

Callum shook his head slowly. 'No. Inside this house is the only place I feel safe.'

'Wow,' Melissa repeated with feeling.

Callum was a little perplexed at her eagerness to believe him. 'How come you don't think I'm crazy? It doesn't make any sense – seeing ghosts, seeing the future. And you've only got my word for it.'

'You proved it to me yourself. You stopped me from getting hurt.'

A glimpse of Melissa lying at the foot of the stairs,

her skull shattered, a bloody mess, flashed across Callum's mind. He tried not to react, but she must have read something in his face, because she suddenly went very still.

'Oh my God, it was more than that, wasn't it? You saved my life. You saw that something terrible was going to happen to me and you stopped it happening.'

Callum gritted his teeth and said nothing.

'Didn't you?'

He didn't have the energy to argue with her. His shoulders slumped forwards in defeat.

'You don't want to believe it yourself, do you?' Melissa said suddenly. 'That's why you're so miserable about it. You don't *want* it to be true.'

'I don't understand why you believe it,' Callum said. 'You've got no proof at all. You don't see the ghosts, you don't have the visions, your hands don't start to tingle when something terrible's about to happen.'

'Do they really?' Melissa asked, with intense interest. 'So you can tell if a vision's coming on?'

'I think so.'

'Can you feel it now?' she asked.

'I . . . well . . .'

Callum had never seen Melissa look so determined. She was concentrating on something.

'Are your hands tingling now?' she asked fiercely.

'Yes . . .' Callum stared at Melissa. His fingers were electric with pins and needles. 'Yes, they are – *What are you doing?*'

Then another vision seared into his brain. Melissa's hand in the fire, her head back, screaming in agony, the skin of her fist charred with bubbling blisters . . .

Callum shook his head, trying to shake the horrific image away. But beside him, Melissa was already reaching out towards the hearth. Pushing her hand towards the burning coals.

Without thinking, Callum rolled over on to his side, knocking her off balance. Then he grabbed her hand and held it down.

'You idiot!' Callum gasped. 'What are you doing?'

'You knew!' Melissa crowed triumphantly. 'You stopped me!'

'But you weren't just *thinking* about doing it – you

were going to do it! If I hadn't stopped you, you'd have actually done it!'

Callum thumped her fist down on the floor between them, holding it firmly. Melissa stared back at him, her chin tilted defiantly.

He suddenly realised he had underestimated her. A lot. She was brave, and determined, and for some reason she trusted him – trusted that he could see the future. She'd been willing to risk burning the flesh off her hand to make her point. To prove to Callum, once and for all, what he was. Perhaps someone like that deserved his trust too.

'I said I wanted to help you,' she whispered.

Callum let go of her hand.

'All right.'

Chapter 12

'Hasn't your gran ever said anything? About you being a chime child, I mean. She must know when you were born.'

Callum shook his head. 'People remember the day you were born, not the exact time – or if there was a full moon.'

Melissa hesitated. 'What about your mum's family?'

'They're all in Cornwall. I haven't seen them since she died three years ago . . .' Callum trailed off. He didn't need a vision of the future to know what Melissa would want to know next – how she had died. But he realised he didn't mind telling her. Telling her about the ghosts had been harder.

'I haven't seen them since my mum's funeral,' Callum went on. 'They never liked Dad and they shut Mum out after she married. When Dad left she stayed up north, because she had a good job. She was like me, I guess, a bit of a loner – an outdoor type. I suppose that's where I get it. She was into mountaineering and that sort of thing. She was killed on a climbing trip in Wales along with three other people. I was supposed to go too, but that morning I decided to play cricket instead.'

'Must be the worst thing ever, losing your mum.'

'Well, you learn to live with it. But I still miss her.'

Melissa hesitated. 'When you see ghosts, do you –'

'No.'

'I wondered if maybe you could ask when you were born.'

Callum shook his head. 'I've never seen her. Besides, I can't talk to ghosts. Most of the time they don't even know I'm there.'

Most of the time.

The conversation came to an awkward halt.

'I know!' said Melissa suddenly. 'The time when you were born must be on your birth certificate.'

'Maybe,' admitted Callum. 'But I've no idea where it is. Besides, we don't need a piece of paper to say I'm a chime child. I think you've already proved that. And I don't think Gran would be convinced anyway. She doesn't believe in magic or anything like that.'

'All the kids at school say she's a witch!' Melissa blurted suddenly, her big eyes very wide again.

'Well, they say that about you too,' Callum retorted. It was true, and Melissa must have known it. 'And they say she's a gypsy, which is rubbish, and they say Mr Gower has an artificial leg, which I bet is also rubbish.'

'You can sort of see why people might think your gran's a witch,' argued Melissa. 'I mean, living out here in the middle of nowhere with only you and the cat.'

'Having a cat doesn't make her a witch, any more than wearing crystals makes you one!' Callum snapped. 'She doesn't know a thing about the supernatural – after I saw the Grim I asked her if there were any local legends about Marlock and she

119

told me to look at a book of old photos of Stockport!'

'Sounds like she's in denial,' said Melissa. 'A bit like you. Or else she's hiding something.'

Callum squirmed uncomfortably. He hadn't forgotten how strangely interested Gran had been when he told her about being followed by the Church Grim, even though she'd tried to explain it away. And then there was the crumbling black and silver book hidden on the ledge above the window . . .

'Don't go in for a career in MI6,' Melissa said. 'Because your poker face is rubbish. What are you thinking about?'

'Books,' admitted Callum, tracing his fingertips over the *Dictionary of the Supernatural*.

Melissa looked around the room. 'You said your gran was only into gardening books and novels. Does she have other books here?'

'I've only seen one,' Callum admitted. 'But yes. She was looking at it last night. She keeps it hidden. I saw her taking it down to have a look at it.'

'Were you asking her about the Grim last night? Maybe that's what she was looking up!'

Callum jumped to his feet and dragged a straight-backed chair over to the window.

'She won't be home for another hour,' he explained. 'The book's up here. She hides it behind this front row of newer stuff. Come and help – we've got to keep track of what we move, because she's bound to notice if they're not put back in the same way. You wouldn't believe how organised she is.'

Melissa scrambled to her feet as well and studied one of the lower shelves for a moment.

'You're right. She's got all these novels arranged in alphabetical order by author. Did she used to be a librarian?'

Callum didn't answer. He was already standing on the chair and pulling books off the high shelf.

'Here, take these,' he said. 'Stack them on the floor by the door. In the exact order I pass them to you.' Much as he was growing to like Melissa, he didn't quite trust her not to make as much of a mess with the books as she'd made with the hot chocolate. 'OK, now I've got another load . . .'

Bit by bit, Callum emptied the shelf. Just as he had

thought, the top shelf was double depth, the books at the front concealing the extra space behind. But it was too dark to see what was there.

'Can you turn the big light on?' he asked, pointing. 'That switch.'

Melissa flicked the switch. Light flooded the room. The telltale flash of silver glimmered from the depths of the hidden shelf, and Callum gasped.

There wasn't just one book back there. There were dozens.

All the books were bound in leather, but there the similarity ended. They were all different sizes, from small notebooks to thick, chunky tomes. Very few had anything legible written on their spines – either the letters had worn away or they had been blank to begin with – so it was impossible to tell what they were. But one thing was certain: hidden behind Gran's discarded gardening journals was a row of books as old as the crumbling alms cottage itself. Maybe even older.

'Is it up there?' Melissa asked, craning her neck to see.

'I can't tell,' said Callum. 'She's got a whole shelf of them here.'

The books were wedged so tightly together, Callum had to pull out a short, fat one to make himself some slack. It was bound in thick, cracked leather, like an old Bible.

'What do you make of this?' he asked, passing it down to Melissa.

'*Campanalogia* – 1677,' she announced, peeking inside the front cover. 'It's all about the secrets of ringing church bells.'

'This is more like it,' said Callum, pulling down another. He opened it and found it was entirely handwritten in painstaking eighteenth-century script.

'What is it?' Melissa asked.

'Hard to tell – the writing's awful. It looks like a collection of stories, though. Fairy stories or something.'

'Well, your gran was obviously telling porkies when she said she didn't have any books about folklore,' Melissa said. 'Can you see the one she was reading yesterday?'

Callum frowned, his eyes skimming over the spines.

'No, I can't. Hang on a sec, it must be here. It was a black book with silver binding.'

It wasn't easy to find. Gran had double-hidden it, laying it flat against the wall behind the row of old books. Callum only noticed it when he pulled a third book off the shelf.

'Got it,' he said triumphantly.

It was heavy. Callum handed the book to Melissa carefully, holding it with two hands. It was wider than it was tall, and fat as a photograph album, but so old it looked as though it ought to be under glass in the British Library. The leather of the cover was slightly greasy with ancient mildew.

Callum hopped down from the chair and laid the book carefully on the drop-leaf table. He wiped his hands before opening the book's heavy black cover. He and Melissa sat side by side and stared at the strange pages.

It was some sort of compendium of legendary creatures, made up of handwritten and pasted-in entries, like a scrapbook. Some of the collection was obviously hundreds of years old. The most ancient entries weren't even on paper, but on thick, crackling parchment or thin skin, sewn on to pages of stiff linen cloth. Generations of collectors must have contributed to it.

'This beats your *Dictionary of the Supernatural*,' Callum breathed.

'Is there an index? How do we look something up?' Melissa asked.

'I don't think you can,' Callum said. 'See – it isn't organised at all. The oldest entries are at the beginning. We'll just have to go through it and see what we find.'

Neither Callum nor Melissa could make sense of the early entries, which were easily four hundred years old. The writing was faded and spiky, in Old English – some of it in Latin. There were drawings, too, of monstrous creatures emerging from tombstones and tree stumps, or rising out of chimneys and wells. One picture showed a thin, hairy creature, like a werewolf, with its stomach cut open. Three dead babies lay inside it. Melissa turned the heavy page over quickly.

Callum stared at the strange collection, astonished. Where in the world had Gran got this, and why did she keep it? Some of the pictures made him want to be sick. The book was like something from another world

– a world which Callum had assumed his down-to-earth, no-nonsense grandmother neither knew nor cared about.

As they turned the pages, the entries became easier to read. Some of the sewn-in pictures were printed broadsheets; some were torn from other books; some were handmade sketches. One, of a strange, brown, leafy creature, was embroidered directly on to the linen page with thin, shining threads.

'Wow, that looks like *hair*,' Melissa said, and peered at the page up close. After a moment she announced triumphantly, 'It *is* hair. The whole picture's made of *human hair*.'

'Ugh,' Callum said, startled but impressed by her boldness. 'Don't touch it. You don't know where it's been.'

Even Melissa did not recognise the forgotten names of some of the strange beings in this old, haphazard catalogue. The Great Horned Woman of Gaughall, Peg Powler and Jenny Greenteeth, the Duergar, Jack-in-Irons, the Mostyn Dragon – page after page of ghosts and demons and spirits, some malignant, some benign.

'There might be something more recent towards the back,' Callum said. 'Skip forwards a bit.'

Melissa turned over a sheaf of stiff linen and the scrapbook fell open to a page full of faded brown photographs on thin glass plates with metal backing. There were six on each side of the page, each photo showing nothing but a haunting woodland scene of bare, tangled trees.

Each picture was simply labelled 'Marlock Wood', in neat, Victorian script, the ink faded as brown as the photographs. Callum turned the page. Another dozen slides of the same view were stuck on the yellowed linen.

Melissa shivered. 'These are spookier than the monsters,' she said. 'The same picture again and again with nothing in it. It's like someone was trying . . .'

' . . .to take a picture of something that doesn't turn up on the film,' Callum finished. 'Yeah. I wonder . . .'

He turned another page, and this time there were twelve pictures all lined up neatly and labelled 'Nether Marlock churchyard'.

This time it was Callum's turn to shiver.

'Nothing in these, either,' said Melissa. 'Unless you count empty graves.'

Callum shook his head. 'It's the photos that are empty, not the graves.'

He turned the next page. He could tell by the weight of the linen that there were no more photos. This time there was a picture – a pen and ink sketch of two figures in a landscape.

The background scene was unmistakeable – it was Nether Marlock Churchyard, seen from exactly the same angle as the photographs, with the old yew tree in the background. Standing in the foreground were a boy and a dog.

The boy was drawn in stark contrasts: dark, longish hair, his tight-fitting Victorian clothes black as well, and a face as pale and blank as a field of snow. The dog beside the boy, crouched as though it were about to spring out of the page, was so big it still came up to his waist. Its fangs gleamed stark white in the black, impenetrable ink of its fur.

The picture was labelled 'The Grim of Nether Marlock churchyard'. Judging by the yellowed paper and faded ink, it was at least a century old. But the boy that looked out from the page was, without doubt, the same one that Callum had forbidden to enter the cottage not quite an hour ago.

It was a picture of Jacob and Doom.

Chapter 13

Beneath the picture was a handwritten note on lined jotter paper. The handwriting was different to any of the other notes or entries they had seen in the book. Callum wondered how many different hands this book had passed through over the hundreds of years of its existence.

This sketch believed to be made by a local shopkeeper known to the photographer, the note read. *After months of failed attempts to capture an image of the Grim with collodion and silver nitrate, this drawing was completed based on an accurate description given to the artist. No more accurate representation is known. The drawing dates to the latter years of the 90s.*

'It's older than that!' exclaimed Melissa.

'It means 1890s, not 1990s,' replied Callum. 'Look how old the photos are. They're on *glass plates*.'

'Is that what your black dog looks like?' Melissa asked.

'That *is* my black dog,' Callum breathed. 'That's the exact place I saw it, beneath that yew tree. Only I saw it there yesterday!'

And outside the door an hour ago, he added silently.

Callum turned another page, but now the entries moved on to more recent photographs of other churchyards, and other stories. Then, towards the back of the book, the entries suddenly skipped forward in time and became more or less contemporary. The dates on the yellowed newsprint were no more than thirteen or fourteen years old. Melissa and Callum both recognised the style of the local weekly newspaper, the *Marlock Advertiser*, which hadn't changed much in the last twenty years.

Haunted Church Out of Bounds This Halloween, read the headline.

Nether Marlock Church, now an ancient monument, will

be surrounded by a police patrol this year over the weekend of 31st October – 1st November. Due to reports of the graveyard being home to a ghostly black dog, Nether Marlock Church has recently become a popular site for Halloween visits. The Advertiser *would like to remind readers in the strongest possible terms that ancient monuments can be dangerous. Under no circumstances should this site be visited in the dark, due to uneven ground and the danger of falling masonry. Police officers will be on hand this weekend to remove any trespassers.*

Beneath this clipping was another note, a careless scrawl written in blue biro.

Others have seen it too. Who reports these sightings? A record of names will amount to a list of local chime births.

On the opposite page was a photocopied leaflet advertising a themed 'Spooky Saturday' at a local pub. The sketch that decorated the advert, a silhouette of a huge dog, looked very familiar. The owner of the blue ballpoint pen clearly thought so too and had commented: *Definitely another recent sighting. Artist unwilling to discuss.*

'Is this your gran's handwriting?' Melissa asked, awed.

'No,' Callum answered. 'It's similar, but hers isn't this spiky.'

As Melissa opened her mouth to reply, Callum heard the click of the front gate. He glanced up wildly at the clock – half past six.

'Quick!' Callum hissed. 'It's Gran! This has to go back on the shelf. We've got a minute if we're quick. I put the bolt on –'

He glanced across at the door. The bolt was drawn back. Callum swore. He'd only bolted it against Jacob, not a second time when Melissa had come in.

'Hurry!'

Melissa hauled her chair across the room and jumped on it in one frantic sweep of energy. Callum handed the book up to her and she slid it into place behind the back row of books.

'Here,' Callum gasped, pressing the gardening books into her arms. 'They've got to be in the right order. Quick, *quick!*'

Gran was struggling with the door. Even without

133

the bolt, it was still double-locked, and that gave them precious extra seconds. Callum shoved the books into Melissa's hands and she banged them into place.

'Callum?' called Gran.

'Wait a sec, Gran, I'm coming!' Callum stalled.

He gave it ten seconds – just long enough for Melissa to slam the last handful of books into place and leap down from the chair.

'Coming, Gran!' Callum cried out breathlessly, and opened the door.

'Why on Earth did you double-lock the door if you were inside, Callum?' asked Gran irritably as she stepped inside. 'There's absolutely no need to –'

She broke off as she surveyed the scene. Callum, red-faced and breathing hard; Melissa standing guiltily beside the chair that she'd pushed haphazardly up against the wall beneath the window.

Melissa gave Gran a nervous smile.

'Hi, Mrs Scott. I'm Melissa Roper from Callum's school. I came to help him with some questions he'd asked about our geography homework –'

'So what are you doing with my books?' Gran asked, jerking the chair away from the wall.

'I was just, um, closing the curtains,' Melissa improvised.

'They were closed,' Gran said stonily.

'Gosh, I'm sorry, Mrs Scott,' Melissa stammered. 'I thought there was a draught. I was just trying to get them shut properly before we started. Sorry about the mess . . .'

Cadbury had found the half-filled mugs still sitting on the hearth and was lapping cold hot chocolate out of one of them. Melissa swooped down to push the cat away but only managed to knock over the mug and spill the remaining contents on to the oriental rug. Cadbury tucked in happily.

'Sorry!' Melissa cringed, mopping at the rug with her sleeve. 'I'm so, so sorry!'

'Never mind that,' snapped Gran. 'Just don't touch anything else! In fact, I think you'd better leave. Do your parents know where you are?'

Gran must have made a direct hit. Melissa winced. 'I was going to ring my mum but I forgot,' she stammered, gathering up her bag and books in a rush. 'I'm sorry. I'll go.'

Gran turned her wrath on Callum. 'I'd like to know ahead of time if you're planning to invite friends round when I'm not here,' she growled. 'I can't have strangers making themselves at home behind my back like this! What were you thinking, Callum?'

'It won't happen again, Mrs Scott,' said Melissa, scooping up her green cape. 'I'll be sure to let you know ahead of time . . .'

'We'll see about that,' was Gran's frosty reply as she stood aside from the still-open door.

Melissa backed out murmuring apologies and excuses. Gran accepted them with a curt nod of her head. She didn't speak as she shut the door.

'Gran! Melissa came here to help me!'

Callum couldn't believe how hostile his gran was being. He couldn't even make sense of it.

'She can help you without going near my books!' Gran snapped.

'Since when did your books become so precious? You never even look at most of them! I haven't had anyone from school round since I came to live here. No one'll come back if you scare them all off. Is that what you want?'

'Oh, Callum, don't be so melodramatic.'

'I'm going to say goodbye,' said Callum. 'Someone told me that was called manners. Oh yeah – it was you.'

With that, Callum yanked open the door and followed Melissa into the darkness.

*

The Hunter is suddenly aware of its prey again.

The Hunter has never known such a thing to happen. It hesitates for a moment, wondering what this means.

No matter; the tantalising trace of power is strong again. The aura that the boy throws off makes the Hunter sigh with anticipation. It will feed soon.

Its quarry is very near. Tormented with hunger, the Hunter closes in.

*

'Melissa, wait!'

Melissa was just closing the gate. She turned and looked back at Callum. Her big eyes and loose, thick hair made her face seem small in the dim light cast by the bulb hanging over the cottage porch.

'I'm really sorry about this,' Callum said awkwardly. 'I don't know what's the matter with her. She's not normally so unfriendly.' He took a breath. 'She's nice, really.'

'Oh, it's OK,' Melissa said. 'I *was* messing with her books, wasn't I? And she hasn't ever seen me before.' Melissa frowned. 'But something really strange is going on here, and your gran knows something about it. We need to find out more about this Churchyard Grim.'

'We'll figure something out,' Callum said quietly. 'And thanks for coming down here on your own. I don't . . . I don't want to get you in trouble.'

Callum's voice trailed away. He didn't want to put her in any *danger*, but he didn't like to say so. Was he dangerous – was it dangerous for him to make new friends? Callum pushed the thought to the back of his mind. He'd been holding people at arm's length for so long he'd never realised how nice it was just to spend time with someone his own age without running around on a sports field.

'We should try to be a bit more methodical about this,' Melissa said. 'We've got the same morning break tomorrow, right? Let's talk about it then.'

She hesitated. 'I don't suppose you could bring that book? We could use the copying machine in the school library –'

Callum shook his head. 'I don't think so. You saw what Gran was like when she noticed you standing near that shelf. I don't know how I'd get to it again without her knowing. It's such a little house.'

'I like it,' Melissa said. 'I love how everything fits together so neatly, like a caravan. Or a narrowboat.'

'Well, it's not much good for keeping secrets in,' Callum replied.

Although Gran seems to have managed, he thought.

Melissa nodded sympathetically. 'Maybe we can find some references to your Churchyard Grim on our own. Let's meet in the school library anyway and do some real research. Libraries keep archives of old newspapers, right? Maybe we can find a copy of that article from the *Advertiser*. Or even something more recent, now we know we've got a local ghost to look for. It might be worth checking the Internet too.'

'That's a good idea,' Callum agreed. 'And I'd like to find out more about what it means to be a chime child. Maybe there's some reason for all this that I'm missing.'

'Don't worry, we'll find something.' Melissa shifted her big mirrored bag so it hung more comfortably over her shoulder. 'See you tomorrow then.'

'Be careful when you get to the estate at the top of the hill, OK? Ed Bolton's been waiting there for me for the last two days, and I bet he'd have a go at you instead if he got the chance.'

'Don't worry. My auntie and all my cousins live up there too. I'll stand on someone's doorstep and scream my head off if he tries anything. And I don't have far to go after that; we live in the yellow-brick house next to the station.'

'Be careful anyway,' Callum said.

'Sure,' Melissa said, nodding.

Callum watched as she walked away into the trees, then took a deep breath and turned back towards the cottage.

Time to face the music.

*

The Hunter's insides twist with hunger.

It can see its prey now, so close, so close — radiant with nourishing power. The sensation makes the Hunter almost dizzy. It halts silently at the garden gate, poised for the kill.

Then the boy steps squarely over the threshold of his dwelling place. Instantly, the tantalising presence vanishes.

The Hunter is baffled. One second it could sense flesh and blood and bone, ripe for the taking. Now it has disappeared behind the crumbling mortar walls as though it never was.

The dwelling must be protected. A charm? Blessing? Curse?

The Hunter slinks around the flimsy barriers thrown

up against mortal intruders: the low wall, the wooden gate, the briar hedge. It leaps lightly along the roof of the adjoining cottage to examine the dwelling from above.

No mere charm protects this place. It is enmeshed in a complex web of magic shields, cloaking it and guarding it. The flowers and herbs along the garden path, the guardian trees, are situated with accurate detail and woven together with spells of warding and concealment. The prey is well protected in its den.

The Hunter pauses. Has this quarry woven this protective web itself? Can it be a foe with power that can be used *against* the Hunter?

The Hunter considers the possibility for a moment.

No. It cannot be. This victim is not dangerous; it is simply better at concealing itself than the others.

But the Hunter knows that a mortal creature cannot stay forever within protective walls. It must venture out for food and the social gatherings that fill all human days. Sooner or later the boy will cross his charmed threshold and stand blinking and unshielded in the world beyond the garden wall.

The Hunter will be waiting. It looks forward to toying with this prey when it is finally caught. An end to this game of cat and mouse.

It is still hungry.

Chapter 14

Gran was on her knees, scrubbing at the spilled hot chocolate with a floor cloth and a steaming bucket of soapy water. As Callum came in she leaned back on her heels and said sarcastically, 'How good of you to join me!'

For once Callum had no doubt that he held the moral high ground. He stood with his hands on his hips and did not offer to help.

'Gran, you were completely unfair to Melissa. You didn't even listen to what she was doing here, you just told her to get out! Is that how you expect me to treat your visitors?'

'Callum, this is *my house*,' Gran retorted angrily. 'I won't have strange teenagers moving my furniture around and making free with my kitchen. I simply won't have it, Callum. You ask first.'

'You weren't here and I didn't know she was coming.'

'All the more reason not to let her in.'

Gran was being completely irrational.

'Gran, Melissa goes to my school. I see her every day. She's in my class. She's not a stranger!'

Gran took a deep breath, obviously trying to control her temper.

'How much do you actually know about this girl?' she challenged. 'Do you know where she lives?'

'The yellow-brick house next to the station,' Callum answered triumphantly.

'Do you know who she lives with? Are her parents still together? Has she got any brothers or sisters?'

'She's got cousins who live in the new housing estate up the hill.'

'I asked about *her*, not her cousins.'

Callum ground his teeth with frustration. 'Gran,

145

look, I don't know those things about her. She doesn't know those things about me, either, except what I told her this afternoon. Those aren't things that matter about a person. The things that matter, you'd like. Melissa's clever. She does well in school, and the teachers like her. She reads all the time, she loves books. And she's –'

Callum remembered how Melissa had nearly put her hand in the fire. He wasn't sure he could call her honest or loyal, but he knew that she was brave and trusting. And something, his Luck maybe, told him that she was *genuine*. She really did want to help him.

But he'd hesitated too long over the right word. Gran interrupted sharply.

'The best thing you could do for a friend like that is try to straighten her out. What was she wearing? All that alternative fashion nonsense, crystals hanging around her neck, those silly tattoos! All she needs is a few paper charms pinned to her skirt. I'll bet she calls herself a Wiccan. What's she trying to be, some kind of witch? You watch out, Callum –'

Callum was so angry he didn't wait to hear the rest

of Gran's tirade. Shoving the drop-leaf table out of the way, he grabbed his homework and stormed upstairs.

*

The impact of his dramatic departure was somewhat lessened when Callum had to come back down to make tea. He'd forgotten it was his turn, and he knew that even after a row, Gran would be expecting him to stick to the routine. If he didn't, there would be no supper at all.

He clattered around in the kitchen, making as much noise as possible. Then they ate a silent meal together. There had never been such a frosty atmosphere between them. If the cottage was too small to keep secrets in, it was even more cramped when you were sharing it with an enemy.

After tea, Callum marched back upstairs and spent the evening in his room. Sitting alone in the cold for a couple of hours made him realise how pleasant it really was sharing the fireside with Gran on a windy November evening.

At last, Gran went to bed too. There was no shifting of furniture tonight; maybe she suspected Callum might still be awake and didn't want to risk giving away the location of her hidden occult library. Despite her reaction to Melissa, Callum didn't think Gran suspected he might have discovered it.

The books . . . As he turned the thought of them over and over in his mind, Callum was only half aware of Gran getting ready for bed next door. The books held answers, he was sure of it. Answers she seemed determined to keep from him. The idea of all that knowledge sitting downstairs, just waiting to be discovered, was torture. What he had said to Melissa was true – he couldn't risk moving any of the books out of the cottage. But that didn't mean he couldn't take another look at them. If he was careful . . .

His mind made up, Callum counted to two thousand after Gran's light went out before he dared to move. Cadbury sighed in displeasure at another midnight disturbance, then got up and stretched. For a moment, Callum was afraid the cat was going to come downstairs with him and get in his way. Shutting him in the bedroom wasn't an option, as Cadbury was bound to yowl for the door to be opened. But instead of following Callum to the door, the cat leaped across to his post on the windowsill and stared out into the darkness. Then he gave a low, rumbling growl of warning.

'What's going on out there?' Callum whispered. 'You're making me nervous, Cad.'

The growl was a sound Callum rarely heard from Cadbury. The cat did lunatic acrobatics sometimes, and Callum was permanently at war with him over the number of dead birds left on the patio, but Cadbury had an easygoing and friendly nature. The strange growling was totally out of character. Callum shivered.

'Just keep it down and don't wake Gran,' he told Cadbury as he slipped through the door on to the tiny landing. It was pitch dark. He tiptoed to the top of the stairs and slowly made his way down, every floorboard in every step creaking as he went. Again Callum had forgotten to put on socks or slippers, and again his feet were freezing. His hands too.

Is it just the cold? he wondered. *Or is something bad about to happen?*

He gave himself a test by dragging one finger hard along a rough timber beam in the stair wall. A sharp pain stabbed underneath his skin. Callum gasped and bit his lip; he'd picked up a splinter on the old wood.

But at least he could feel his fingertips. No visions tonight, then.

Callum made it to the bottom of the stairs without waking Gran, and for a moment stood still, breathing slowly while his heart pounded. He'd have to pull himself together if he wanted to find the old scrapbook again.

There was a faint red glow coming from the grate, just enough to see by. When he'd managed to get his breathing back to normal, Callum quietly lifted one of the straight-backed chairs and carried it to the window. He knew where to look now; he wouldn't have to move too many books before he found the one he wanted. Maybe he *could* manage to sneak the ancient scrapbook into his rucksack, get it to school and make copies of the picture of Jacob. Or maybe he could just take the picture with him and leave the book in its usual place. That would be safer.

Callum paused, just in case he'd disturbed Gran's sleep when he was creeping downstairs, or she'd stirred while he was moving the chair. These days Callum knew all too well what it was like to lie awake in the dark, straining to hear something out of the ordinary.

The night was silent. Almost too quiet. There was no wind, and no sound from outside. Even the owls seemed to have lost their voices, and Callum felt the hair at the back of his neck rise. It was like the feeling he'd had in his dream, when he had come to the path beside the canal – a sensation of dread, the sure knowledge of the presence of evil. Only, at the canal he had known that the evil was in the past, over and done with. This was entirely more urgent. There was evil here *now*. It was beyond the cottage walls, but it was close – too close. In the garden perhaps, waiting and lurking, a thing old and full of malevolence.

Had Jacob come back? Callum had shut him out once, but he was sure the ghost boy wasn't going to give up. Could he be out there now, prowling with his demon hound? All Callum's body was prickling now with the sensation of danger, not just his fingers. Was the danger all around the house? Callum closed his eyes and allowed the unfamiliar sense to guide him. No, it was worse at the back. He could feel it there, sense it as though it were calling him. It was in the back garden.

Next to the doorway leading to the little kitchen, the wall of the sitting room had a set of full-length glass doors that opened on to the garden. Callum crossed to them and quietly pulled open one of the curtains so he could look outside.

The sky had cleared. The garden was awash in silver moonlight and blue shadows. Callum didn't know what he expected to see. Anything out of the ordinary would have startled him, even a fox crossing the garden, but all seemed peaceful. Nothing stirred, but the tingling in Callum's body was stronger than ever. He scanned the night again and his heart turned over with a thump of shock.

Someone was standing at the far end of the garden.

Callum could not make out any features, but he felt sure it wasn't Jacob. It was not anyone or anything he had seen before. It was thin and spindle-shanked, a black stick-figure silhouetted in the bright moonlight. It might have been a leafless tree, except that no tree had ever stood there before. Callum's mouth went dry as he realised that the shadowy figure was inside, not outside, the low garden wall.

Then, as he watched, the figure began to make its way slowly up the winding brick path towards the cottage.

With every step, fear tightened its grip on Callum. The moonlight was so bright it threw long shadows from Gran's plum trees and bird table, but the moving figure cast no shadow of its own. It was halfway to the house now, and Callum still couldn't make out anything about it, except that its body seemed to be glistening wet. Callum watched, appalled and fascinated, his hair on end. The thing was not human, but it wasn't a ghost. It was something *else*.

The dark figure came closer. Callum wanted to flee, but could only stand transfixed with horror. What was the point in running upstairs and hiding his head under the duvet, with something like this waiting for him outside the cottage walls?

The figure had reached the patio. It walked slowly across the stone slabs and stood at the glass door directly in front of Callum, confronting him.

It was shaped like a human. But it had no face.

Its head was a mass of wet, gleaming veins and cartilage, muscle and teeth – a face without skin or form; lipless, lidless, without nose or ears. It was a flayed face, a face that had been peeled of skin and laid bare. The creature held Callum's gaze with its unblinking eyes. Callum, frozen in terror, dared not look away.

They stood only a foot apart, staring at each other, nothing between them but the thin panes of the old glass door. The thing tilted its glistening head with what seemed to be an arrogant, mocking curiosity.

And then the hideous face changed.

Before Callum's eyes, human skin grew over the naked web of veins. A human face knitted itself over the bloody flesh. The staring eyes grew lids and lashes, lips grew full and hid the grinning white teeth. Hair sprouted from the gleaming skull.

The change happened in seconds. But the moment Callum realised what he was looking at seemed to go on for hours.

On the other side of the glass door stood a boy of medium height and rugged build in his early teens. There was nothing eerie about this boy, apart from the fact that seconds earlier he had been a monster. Callum saw a face with broad cheekbones and tangled brown hair that was too long and standing up at the back. The face looked a little anxious around the eyes, with a crease of worry between the eyebrows. But it was just a face. A normal face.

It was *his* face.

Callum stood trembling in the dark, staring through the glass at a perfect replica of himself, even down to the expression of wide-eyed horror and revulsion. It was as if the creature was giving Callum a moment to realise what he was seeing.

Beware the dark reflection . . .

The creature that was not Callum moved suddenly, reaching for the handle of the door. Callum met the movement frantically, grabbing at the handle from the inside to make sure the door was locked – both he and Gran sometimes forgot. Matching hands met on the door handles on opposite sides of the glass and Callum braced himself for a desperate struggle.

At that moment a long, wild howl cut through the silence of the night, deep and powerful and rolling like thunder, and Callum recognised the voice of Doom the Churchyard Grim.

For the first time, the creature outside produced an expression that did not reflect Callum's. Instead, it frowned. It narrowed its eyes, glanced over its shoulder quickly, and took its hand from the door. Its look was cold and angry. Then the thing met his eyes again and smiled.

The smile turned Callum's blood to ice. It was a look of ugly promise and anticipation. But for now, it did nothing more. Slowly, never taking its eyes off Callum's own, the monster backed away down the garden path. Callum noticed that now the thing had taken his face, it cast a shadow too. He shivered.

Finally, with a triumphant, taunting grin, the thing

with Callum's face vanished in the black tangle of trees at the bottom of the garden, as if it had never existed.

Chapter 15

Friday. It was Friday morning, thank God.

Callum trudged wearily through the corridors, hardly noticing the other kids that rushed past on either side of him, laughing and joking. His body might have been in Marlock High School, but his mind was still trapped in the moonlit cottage garden. His brain seemed stuck in a loop, replaying over and over again the terrifying moment when the monster had stolen his face. He had hardly slept, apart from an hour's fitful dozing around dawn. The walk to school had been a waking nightmare – with imaginary monsters lurking behind every tree. But he had made it in one piece, and at least now all he had to do was get through one day of school and then he had the weekend to try to figure out what was happening to him – and how to stop it.

'Bolton's looking for you, Scott,' Baz hissed in Callum's ear on the way into English.

Typical. As if he didn't have enough to worry about without having to avoid Ed Bolton – who, Callum imagined, had not spent the evening chasing ghosts and demons out of his garden. No, Ed had probably been sleeping soundly, dreaming of what he would do to Callum when he finally caught up with him. Because this morning, he was definitely on the prowl.

Callum barely avoided him between lessons, ducking into an empty classroom at the last minute as Ed marched past, his beady eyes scanning the crowd. In the middle of history, Melissa passed Callum a note which said, *Don't go to the canteen at break. Heard Ed making plans to come and find you there. Meet me in the library.*

She dropped the message on Callum's desk with such cool and quiet calm that Callum was sure no one could possibly have noticed. He was impressed by her yet again.

Then, after the lesson, Callum went to his locker and found a fearsome scrawl of tomato sauce still dripping down the door. Ed's DIY decorating job was simple and ugly, but the message to Callum was crystal clear. It also brought back, harsh and sharp, the shocking bloody message of his dream, and Jacob's warning.

'Bolton's stylish signature, right?' said Hugh Mayes sympathetically as he arrived at his own locker. 'Want a hand, Scott?'

'Thanks, but you're better off out of it,' Callum said. He shook his scruffy hair out of his face and went to get a paper towel to wipe away the mess before one of the teachers saw it. Never in all his life had a school day dragged so slowly.

Just as there were more ghosts on the streets of Marlock lately, they also seemed to have multiplied in the halls of Marlock High School that morning. Callum saw one that must be hundreds of years older than the school itself; a man in a homemade peasant smock digging what looked like a grave outside the gym. Even from a distance, Callum could see that the man's face was covered in sores, like a plague victim, and the cold wind that seemed to swirl about him carried the faint scent of rotten flesh.

Why were there so many of them? Why now? Callum smashed his fist against his locker in frustration, prompting a hail of giggles from a group of year seven girls on their way to lessons. Owen, the rugby team captain, slapped Callum lightly on the back. 'Cool it, Scott. Nearly the weekend!' Callum nodded and forced a smile. He didn't want to draw attention to himself. He didn't want Ed to notice him.

Callum made his way quietly to the school library. Melissa was waiting for him at one of the tables, books already stacked in front of her. She looked up as Callum came in and shrugged her shoulders sadly.

'There's a ton of stuff here about Cheshire during World War Two. But nothing about chime children. Or big black dog ghosts. You didn't manage to bring your gran's scrapbook, did you?'

'No such luck,' said Callum, shifting awkwardly. 'I, er, couldn't get to it.'

Truth be told, he had completely forgotten about the old book. Although it was less than a day since they had found the hidden library, the excitement of that discovery had been completely blotted out by the late-night prowler. He shivered at the memory of the moonlight glistening on its skinless body, and Melissa gave him a curious look, widening her big eyes in a wordless question.

Callum tried to excuse himself.

'I'm totally spooked by all this.'

'Yeah, I can see why. And I guess you're not telling me the whole story, either.'

'Have you tried the obvious?' Callum asked, ignoring Melissa's probing comment. 'Have you tried looking up "chime child" on the Internet?'

'Yes I have, Old Smugs, and the school has got blocks and parental controls set so high that I can't even get a search on "ghoul". It won't let me on any sites that have anything to do with the occult. You have to get special permission from the librarian to access the BBC news, for goodness sake.'

'Huh.' Callum frowned. 'Have you got a computer at home?'

'Mum has a laptop from work, but it's about as easy to get hold of as your gran's books. But don't worry. How about we try the local library after school? Computer access is free there, yes I have a library card, and yes they do have user restrictions, but it's not as bad as here. Plus they probably have back issues of the *Advertiser* available, and they're much more likely to have a section on local history. The school library is just too general. Not very big, either. I could meet you at the end of the day . . .'

'Sure,' Callum agreed, wishing he could share her optimism.

He moved to his next class, his skin still crawling, counting the minutes until the school day was over. He couldn't shake the feeling of being watched – of someone standing close behind him, boring into the back of his head with a fixed stare, or falling into step behind him in the halls. And it wasn't Ed's gang who were giving Callum this feeling. They were there, for sure, and watching him. But they weren't being secretive about it. Whenever one of them passed Callum in the hall, they went out of their way to give him a shove with a shoulder or a gym bag; Harry pinged a rubber into the back of his head during maths. No, there was something else.

At lunch, Callum went into the cafeteria at the last possible minute before the hot food finished. He hovered in the doorway for a moment, scanning the faces at the tables. Most were half empty now, and he couldn't see any sign of Ed through the milling crowd. But wait . . . For a split second, Callum thought he saw a glimpse of a familiar face. His pulse quickened. Was it Ed? He craned his neck. Then two year eight girls moved aside and suddenly he could see.

Sitting alone on the other side of the cafeteria, Callum saw himself.

He blinked and looked again. The boy's head was turned away now. Maybe he'd been mistaken.

Then the boy turned back and met his gaze. Callum stood frozen, staring back in disbelief. It was the creature from last night – here in the school, in broad daylight.

As Callum watched, Ed's mate Craig walked past the thing wearing his face, giving it a shove as he went. The creature didn't react. It never took its unblinking eyes off Callum. Its stare was open and mocking, its mouth twisted in the same malevolent smirk it had fixed on its borrowed face the night before.

Callum backed slowly out of the cafeteria. Pins and needles stabbed at his palms as the creature rose to its feet and began crossing the room towards him. He waited for people to realise they were seeing double – to ask themselves how Callum could be in two places at once – but then he realised there was no chance of that. He'd worked too hard to make himself invisible to the other kids at school. They probably hadn't noticed there was even one Callum Scott in the room, let alone two.

The monster was halfway across the cafeteria now, striding confidently forwards. Callum had retreated into the corridor. He looked right and left, his mouth dry. Whatever it was, the creature was coming for him, and this time there was nothing to protect him. There were even fewer people out here, no one to help. He turned on his heel and set off at a fast walk, his shoes squeaking anxiously on the polished floor. Maybe Mr Gower would be in his office . . . Glancing over his shoulder, Callum saw his doppelgänger emerge from the cafeteria. As it caught sight of him, Callum could have sworn he saw its evil smile widen in anticipation.

Callum gritted his teeth. No, whatever this thing was, it wasn't going to be frightened off by the pompous deputy head. He quickened his pace.

Empty classrooms and closed doors whipped past. Callum glanced backwards again. The thing was still there, matching his speed. Maybe even closing in. Callum could see the rest of the school outside, enjoying the late autumn sunshine. He wanted to scream and bang on the windows to attract their attention but he didn't dare stop.

The thing on his heels was closer now. Its eyes gleamed in the shadows of the dimly lit corridor. This corridor was off limits to students, mostly storerooms and old classrooms awaiting refurbishment. Every step was taking Callum farther and farther away from help. With a sudden jolt, he realised that this was what the creature wanted – to get him out of sight. Dread clutched at his heart. He wasn't just being hunted, he was being *herded*.

A staircase was coming up fast on his left. But going up would be suicide. Callum's only hope was to get outside, into the crowd. He felt certain now that the monster wouldn't follow. It wanted to catch him here, where it could do whatever it wanted to him unseen. Hurrying past the stairs, Callum turned a sharp corner.

Into a dead end.

A few metres ahead, the corridor ended in a blank wall. Callum's heart plummeted. He should have taken the stairs when he had the chance. Now he was trapped.

Or was he? At first he hadn't noticed the peculiar ridge running across the wall at waist level. A second later, as his eyes adjusted to the gloom, he could see that the ridge was a narrow metal bar, broken in two in the middle, and that a thin line of light ran down the centre of the wall, like a seam of gold.

It was a door!

Behind him, Callum heard the monster's pursuing footsteps break into a run, as if it had sensed its prey was about to escape. Without hesitating, Callum raced forward himself, as the creature hurtled around the corner behind him.

Throwing his arms forward, Callum slammed his hands into the bar. With a metallic screech, the double doors flew open and Callum stumbled out into the bright sunlight – right into a group of startled first years.

Panting, he spun round. The monster had come to a halt just inside the door. For a moment it glared at Callum, its eyes glowing with fury. Then it turned on its heel and vanished back into the gloomy corridor.

*

Callum thought he saw the thing two or three times again throughout the afternoon – a fleeting glimpse of his own face on the stairs, in the hall, across the playing fields. Even though he made absolutely sure he was never left alone, by the time the last bell rang he had still been reduced to a jangle of nerves. His concentration in lessons was non-existent. He'd even thought about skiving off the end of the day and going home early – but what would be the point? He'd probably escape Ed, but Callum didn't think he'd get away so easily from the creature. There was safety in numbers. Ed certainly wouldn't dare try anything while they were in a crowd, and it seemed that the face-stealing monster was also publicity-shy. Besides, Melissa would be waiting for him when classes were over. He didn't like to think that he might be dragging her into danger, but Callum had to admit he was looking forward to her company.

She was waiting at the gate, staring into the distance as though her mind were very far away, but she snapped right back to reality when she saw Callum.

'Made it safe and sound?' she asked.

'So far,' Callum answered.

'That Ed's a lout. Good thing he's so dim, or he'd be frightening.'

Callum couldn't bring himself to admit that Ed was

the least of his worries. Instead, he nodded with a weak grin.

'Yeah. Let's get moving or he'll catch up with us.'

Hordes of ghosts were clustering in shop doorways and on the footpaths of the town – even more than usual. Melissa couldn't see them, of course. Callum wondered if he ought to describe them to her, and decided against it. No point in making her think he was any weirder than he'd already admitted to being.

'I want to pop into the post office and get a new notebook,' Melissa said. 'Then we can make proper notes.'

'Are you training to be a librarian?'

'Ha ha,' Melissa retorted sarcastically.

Because it was just outside school hours, there was a queue of kids lined up outside the post office – the shopkeeper was being as rigid as always about his 'two schoolchildren at a time' rule. Callum was uncomfortable about hanging about, but a few moments probably wouldn't hurt. They were still in a public place after all. Even if Ed turned up, the shopkeeper wouldn't let a fight take place on his stretch of pavement without calling the police. He'd done it before.

But still, it wasn't easy to stand about in the street when you knew there was a shape-shifting monster tailing you. The tingling in his hands had faded since the nightmare chase through the school corridors, but it hadn't gone away entirely. Callum felt sure that the creature was as hot on his trail as Ed. He looked around as he waited, searching the faces up and down the line of uniformed students. He saw nothing out of the ordinary, no face he didn't recognise, all of them living and none of them his.

Callum wasn't even aware he had heaved another sigh until Melissa patted him kindly on the shoulder.

'Cheer up, it's our turn next.'

The little shop seemed empty after the jostling crowd in the street. Callum slouched by the cold drinks cabinet where he could keep an eye on the kids passing by outside. There was still no sign of Ed, or Callum's phantom double.

'I'm finished,' Melissa said, appearing at his shoulder. She held out a Mars bar. 'Got you a chocolate bar.'

Callum forced a laugh. 'Typical girl – you think chocolate cures everything!'

'Can't hurt. Come on, let's get to the library before the enemy turns up.'

The shopkeeper-turned-bouncer stepped back to let Melissa and Callum past on their way out and beckoned to the next pair of lucky shoppers, growling the unnecessary warning: '*Two*. Two of you only.'

The bell above the door chimed as Callum opened it, and as if in answer, the Friday afternoon was shattered by a piercing scream of agony.

Chapter 16

The Hunter walks among the living crowd, wearing the face of its chosen victim.

Rage burns though its inhuman veins. The Hunter had its prey within its grasp, only for the victim to slip through its fingers again. What is it about this boy? He is different from the others: more cunning, more elusive. And oh, so much more powerful. The Hunter yearns to feed on that power.

It is too hungry to wait any longer. There is another chime child whose nourishing spirit the Hunter can trace. It is not as strong as the boy whose face the Hunter wears. It is one of those weaker beings born close to dawn, hardly aware of their own abilities. It will not be a satisfying meal. But it will strengthen the Hunter for the longer chase to come.

Here, now, the other victim approaches – the feeble, fearless one, escorted by another boy. Its fury still boiling within it, the Hunter confronts the human, smiling its borrowed smile.

'Look! It's Scott, just waiting for you, Ed! And grinning like a dope. Hey Scott, been looking for us?'

'I guess you got my message, Scott,' says the one that will make a nourishing morsel, with a nasty smile of its own. 'Thanks for waiting. You coming for a chat with us? We want to hear about your freaky girlfriend. And your gyppo gran.'

The angry words mean nothing to the Hunter. It can use human speech if such speech serves a purpose, but its purpose now is simply to feed. It savours the moment when its victim stands willingly within reach, so foolishly unafraid.

'Answer me, Scott!'

A fist whips out. The Hunter brushes the flimsy hand aside.

'Come on, Ed, don't do it here. Let's take him along

to the engine shed and give him a kicking.'

The Hunter is too hungry to toy with its prey any longer. In an instant, faster than either of the mortals can react, it attacks. Its claws rake the boy's throat, biting into the warm flesh. Red blood sprays like a fine mist, the salt taste seeking out the Hunter's lips. The boy staggers back, his eyes wide now with terror.

It is almost an invitation.

The Hunter leaps forward. The boy collapses beneath the onslaught. Now the Hunter is on his chest, its talons seeking those glistening orbs, piercing the pupils and sinking into the jelly.

The boy screams once, in terror and agony, as the meal begins.

Chapter 17

Callum and Melissa raced towards the cry.

Why am I running towards *the screaming?* thought Callum fleetingly.

Then he knew. Memory battered him from all sides – the sense of urgency, the terrible shriek of agony suddenly cut short, the knowledge that he had come too late, and –

And a boy lying slouched against the brick wall with dripping bloody holes where his eyes should be.

But not an unknown boy this time.

Ed Bolton.

He lay broken and disfigured, his face a river of

bloody tears leaking from the empty sockets. Ed's second-in-command, Baz, was backed against the wall beside the body. He was weeping his own tears of terror, and he had been sick all over the road. Now he looked up at Callum and started screaming.

'Don't come near me! Don't come near me! Get away from me!'

Paying absolutely no attention, Melissa ran forwards with outstretched arms, instinctively offering help.

'No, no, you crazy witch, get away!'

Baz scrambled backwards away from Melissa, but slipped on his own vomit and went sprawling into the pool of blood that was slowly spreading across the pavement. He screeched again and tried to claw himself to his feet against the wall without having to touch Ed's lifeless body. Melissa reached him and offered her hand; Baz shoved her back into the road. Callum stepped between them.

He glanced swiftly at Ed and felt his own stomach lurch at the sight of the glistening, bloody eye sockets.

How had it happened – in broad daylight, here in Marlock, barely outside the school gates? How? He turned away from Ed's ruined face and asked Baz in desperation, 'What happened?'

'What happened?' Baz repeated wildly, frantically trying to wipe Ed's blood off his hands. 'What do you mean, *what happened?* You freakin' murderer! You killed him!'

Baz stopped suddenly, doubled over in the gutter, and vomited again. Callum drew back, shaking. Melissa grabbed his arm.

'*What* happened?' Melissa whispered.

'Get away from him, you stupid cow! He's a crazy freak, a killer! He jumped him, he jumped right at his face, and he just dug his nails into Ed's head and then he . . . he . . . he *ATE* them! He *ATE* –'

But Baz couldn't bring himself to say it. Instead he tried to vomit again, his empty stomach bringing up nothing but bile as he retched and retched. Finally, gasping, he looked up at Callum and screamed hysterically, 'Just back off, Callum Scott! Just back the hell off!'

By now a crowd was gathering. Callum and Melissa weren't the only ones who had heard the screaming

– first Ed's terrible death agony, and then Baz's hysterical accusations. The crowd was mostly kids, but there were some adults too.

'Get him away from me. He did it – *he* did it!' Baz pointed and shrieked, all his fear and revulsion focused on Callum. 'He went crazy! He ripped Ed's eyes out – ripped them right out of his head. He killed him!'

Weeping, whispering girls and muttering boys crowded the pavement. There were more screams as new people arrived and saw the sickening horror of the scene for the first time. Everybody had a phone. Every one of them was dialling 999. Two separate crowds were forming now, one around the savaged wreck of the body that had once been Ed Bolton, and the other around Callum. Hands grabbed at him, driving him to his knees and pinning his arms behind his back. Through the fog of shock that seemed to have paralysed him, Callum heard conflicting orders flying.

'Tie his arms together!'

'No, you'll get in trouble, doing that to a kid. Wait for the police!'

'Who cares? A lad who does a thing like that? Tie him up, safer for us all that way –'

'Callum didn't do it!'

Melissa had managed to push her way to the front of the mob. Stunned by the fierceness of the crowd, Callum noticed for the first time that one of the men holding him down was Mr Gower, the deputy head. Melissa noticed at exactly the same time.

'Mr Gower! Mr Gower! Listen to me!' she shouted. 'Callum's been with me all afternoon, since school got out! I was waiting for him outside and I've been with him the whole time since! He didn't do anything!'

'You're in it together!' Baz screamed at her. 'You both hated him!'

Melissa ignored Baz completely. She brandished her recently purchased notebook.

'Mr Gower, you've got to listen to me!'

Gower beckoned to another man to come and take his place holding Callum, then got to his feet and drew Melissa aside.

'I know it's hard to accept,' Gower said, 'but sometimes we don't understand –'

'No, *listen!*' Melissa cried. 'We were in the post office. See this?' She held up the notebook. 'We just bought it. We were in the queue for fifteen minutes with tons of other kids. Then we were in the shop. We only heard the screaming as we came out! We've got *dozens* of witnesses. Ask any of them! Callum didn't do it!'

'Well, we can check,' said Gower dubiously. 'But that's up to the authorities.'

Right on cue, wailing sirens and flashing lights began to pull up around them. It was emergency vehicle overkill – a couple of ambulances, a police van and at least three squad cars. Dazed as he was, Callum couldn't see through the crowd to count them all. A medical team swooped down on Ed's lifeless body and a swarm of uniformed police officers began to organise the crowd. Baz was gently coaxed into one of the police cars so he could make a statement. At this point the policemen noticed Callum, nailed to the ground by half a dozen men.

'This the suspect?'

Melissa was as persistent as a bulldog. Since she'd

got no joy from the deputy head, she shifted her focus to the police officers.

'Callum Scott didn't do this! I was with him all afternoon. We were in the queue outside the post office! You can ask anyone who was there. And there's CCTV, too. You can check that. You can check!'

She wasn't hysterical, she was dogged. But she couldn't stop the officers hauling Callum to his feet, frisking him against the wall, and snapping handcuffs into place around his wrists. She finally got through to one of the junior officers who was taking notes and looking for witnesses.

'CCTV in the corner shop. Right, we'll check that. There's a camera at the school gate, too.' The brisk young woman swivelled on her heel and pointed with her pen. 'Anyone from the school here now? Teachers, I mean.'

'The deputy head there – the bald guy,' Melissa gasped gratefully. 'Mr Gower.'

'Right-o. I'll speak to him.' The officer scribbled his name down. 'And your name, miss?'

'Melissa Roper.'

'Are you one of the victim's friends?' the policewoman asked kindly.

'No!' Melissa's answer was forceful. 'No, I wasn't. He was a bully. But . . .' Callum saw her staring woefully at the policewoman with her big, soulful eyes opened wide. 'But what happened to Ed shouldn't happen to anyone. And there isn't a girl or a boy in the school who'd do *that*.'

A couple of other kids were gathering round Melissa now. Some of them nodded in agreement with her, but then Ed's mate George shouted, 'Don't pay any attention to Melissa, miss, she's Callum's *girlfriend*!'

'I am not!' Melissa responded angrily.

The officer gave Melissa a quick, sharp look, but continued scribbling on her notepad. 'Telephone number?' she asked.

Callum didn't hear any more of the conversation. He was being frogmarched to the police van by four black-suited officers in protective vests while another two wrestled the heavy doors open. He was still too numb to struggle or even protest.

Just as they got the doors to the van open, Melissa appeared at his side again. She'd forced her way out through the crowd and past the barrier of police surrounding the emergency vehicles.

'Callum!' she cried. 'They're not going to take my word against Baz's, but they'll check the cameras.'

One of the policemen grabbed Melissa by the shoulders and pulled her back. Callum finally came to his senses.

'Tell Gran!' he called out to her.

'What?'

'Go and find my gran. Tell her what happened – tell her where they're taking me!'

Never in his life had Callum been so anxious to have Gran, with her practicality and determination, battling on his side.

'Anything else? Can I do anything else?' Melissa cried out desperately.

'Just tell Gran!'

The strong arms that held him began to lift him into the van. Inside its dark interior, Callum was shoved down on the single hard bench, a policeman on either side of him. Someone pulled a barred gate across the opening with a clang.

Callum heard Melissa's anxious voice calling out one more desperate message to him:

'I'll go and get her now!'

Then the van doors slammed shut.

Chapter 18

The police cell was clinically clean and bare. Callum sat on the narrow mattress with his head in his hands, still dazed, and growing increasingly frightened.

He had not been charged with anything. The term they had used when they locked him up was 'detention before charge'. The Custody Sergeant had been very clear as he explained it. While they decided if there was sufficient evidence to charge him, Callum would be held in custody. If a charge was made, it would be for murder – for the grisly, cold-blooded murder of Ed Bolton.

Callum could scarcely believe that the events of the

past few hours had actually happened. His arrest had gone strictly by the book. He had been taken into Marlock Police Station, photographed, fingerprinted, breathalysed and made to give a urine sample, too – Baz's description of Callum's behaviour had made him sound so thoroughly insane that there was suspicion he might be high on some kind of mind-altering drug. They had taken his clothes for forensic testing, leaving him a pair of white overalls that were at least three sizes too big for him. And he was bombarded with questions – did he have any existing medical conditions? Did he want to speak to a solicitor? Callum couldn't imagine that the ability to see ghosts counted as an existing medical condition, and he didn't think it would be a good idea to mention it. He had been allowed one phone call and had tried to ring Gran. She hadn't answered.

So Callum waited. He sat with his head sunk in his hands. It was all unbelievable. He couldn't think straight. Couldn't get the events of the day ordered in his mind. His brain dragged him relentlessly back to the scene of Ed's murder – to that first terrible moment of discovery, when he had seen his eyeless body . . .

A memory of something Jacob had said popped into Callum's unwilling head.

Surely you have seen it – boys and girls like you, killed.

Chime children, with their eyes torn out.

Could Ed have been a chime child? Now that he thought about it, there was no reason there shouldn't be other chime children in Marlock – Callum wasn't necessarily the *only* child in the town born between midnight on Friday and cockcrow on Saturday on the night of a full moon. The thought had never occurred to him. No one else could see ghosts, could they? Or maybe, like Callum, they just didn't admit it. Jacob had said that Callum was like other chime children, but stronger. Maybe someone like Ed only saw ghosts now and then, and was able to explain it away to himself. Or didn't care. Or hadn't developed the ability before . . .

Before he was killed. Killed horribly, just because of when he was born.

It was Friday now, but only early evening – not yet midnight. Callum wondered feverishly if something would change within him during the chime hours. Would his powers be sharpened, his ability to see ghosts heightened? He tried to remember if there was any pattern to his visions, but he couldn't concentrate on anything further back than the beginning of the week.

And what good would it do if his powers *did* increase after midnight? Another chime child had been killed and Callum hadn't been able to do anything to stop it. Instead, he was being blamed for it. Why *had* Baz insisted Callum was the murderer?

Then Callum's dazed mind came sharply into focus. *What an idiot!*

It was the creature with his face.

That was what was killing the chime children. Not the sinister Jacob, nor his hell hound. The monster had come for Callum in the night, but it had fled when it heard Doom's howling. Thwarted at the cottage, it had come to find him at school. Ed's friend Craig had mistaken the creature for Callum in the cafeteria. After school, Ed must have come looking for him, and got more than he bargained for.

BEWARE THE DARK REFLECTION

Jacob had said it was a warning, but Callum hadn't believed him. He'd been so busy running from the monster that it hadn't occurred to him it might harm someone else. And now, how could he possibly escape a murder charge if the killer was wearing his own face . . .?

Footsteps broke the silence, echoing down the bare corridor outside the cells. Then voices – one deep and authoritative, the other shrill and demanding. Callum raised his head suddenly in wild relief.

Gran.

The harsh echoes made it difficult to make out what she was saying, but she was talking to the Custody Sergeant. It sounded like the policeman was getting a right earful.

With a clank, the cell door opened, and there she was.

'Callum!'

Then she was running to him, and crushing him to her tightly in one of her rare hugs. It had never felt so good.

'You're free, Callum,' she said firmly. 'No more worries.'

Callum jerked back.

'What?'

'That girlfriend of yours is a right bright spark,' the Custody Sergeant said approvingly. 'She was absolutely spot on about the CCTV. You're a very lucky lad. Every step you took since you left school this afternoon is on camera, and you were clearly nowhere near the scene of the crime.'

Callum let out a huge sigh of relief to hear the policeman sounding so convinced and sympathetic.

'It's true that the allegations against you were very serious,' the officer continued, 'but quite apart from the only eyewitness being unreliably hysterical, even without the camera footage there's not a shred of evidence against you. This was a violent crime. It would have left your hands and clothes covered in –'

The Custody Sergeant coughed, clearing his throat at the unpleasant thought of what Callum would have been covered in had he really ripped Ed's eyes out of his skull and eaten them.

'Well, as I said, there's no evidence,' the policeman finished. 'I don't know what did happen, but you obviously had nothing to do with it.'

'What do I do now?' Callum asked faintly.

'Go home with your gran, eat your tea and have a lie-in tomorrow,' the Custody Sergeant said kindly. 'You can leave this case to Greater Manchester's Finest now. It's nothing to do with you any more – though of course you may be called on as a witness.'

'Come on, Callum,' Gran said.

They let him change back into his uniform and gave him back his anorak and rucksack. Then Gran and Callum walked home in silence. It had been dark for some time, and Callum was glad to have Gran's no-nonsense company on the road through Marlock Wood. None of the usual ghosts were hovering there, and the light over the front door of Gran's cottage shone cheeringly through the leafless trees. Callum stood shivering on the path while Gran let them in. They both sat down in their usual armchairs in front of the fire, without even taking off their coats.

'Well, good grief!' Gran exclaimed finally. 'All right

now, Callum. I've heard out the police and I've heard out your friend Melissa Roper. Let's hear *your* side of this awful story.'

'Oh, Gran –' Callum started. He broke off and tried again. 'Was the actual murder caught on CCTV too?'

'No. The camera only gets the car park. It caught you and Melissa running past after you heard the screaming.'

Callum didn't know whether he was relieved or disappointed. He didn't really think the supernatural creature that was after him was any more likely to be caught on film than a ghost was. Yet Baz had seen it. So had Craig, in the dinner hall. Sure, they'd seen the monster when it was in Callum's form, but they'd seen *something*. It was a being that could reveal itself to anyone, not just chime children. Not like a ghost . . .

Gran leaned forwards in her chair. 'So what happened?'

Something in Callum snapped. He just couldn't keep up the pretence, the secrecy of his thirteen years, any longer. He didn't think he should keep it secret now. The world of ghosts and monsters was affecting *his* world – not just him, not just chime children, but everyone. Every boy and girl at Callum's school who had witnessed Ed's defiled body lying on the pavement in a pool of blood. Callum couldn't bear the burden of being the only one who knew what had really happened.

'Gran, I think I know who did it. I mean, *what* did it. It wasn't human.'

Gran sat very quietly. She didn't protest. She seemed to be listening, so Callum went on.

'Last night there was . . . there was a *thing* in the back garden. Like a person, but without a face. I don't know what it was. It came down the garden path and stood at the glass doors and looked at me. And then . . .' Callum paused. Unbelievably, Gran was still listening. Her expression was serious but impossible to read. She didn't interrupt. 'Then it *grew* a face. And the face was mine. The thing looked just like me.'

'Oh, Callum,' said Gran softly. Her voice was full of dismay, but there was no surprise in it, and her expression was understanding.

'I don't know what the thing was, Gran, but it . . . it

wasn't a ghost –' Callum broke off again.

'A ghost?' Gran prompted quietly.

'I can see ghosts too,' Callum admitted. 'I've always been able to, Gran. They're real. And they're everywhere.'

'Can you see them here?' Gran asked seriously. 'Can you see them in this house?'

'No, I can't,' Callum replied. 'But then you already know that, don't you?'

Gran sighed. 'Yes, Callum,' she said softly.

'But you never said anything!'

'People don't like to talk about ghosts, do they?' she answered, her voice edged with something like sadness. 'But if you don't see them here, then what was the thing in the garden?'

'That's what scares me. I don't know what it was. It was something *else*. A monster. It borrowed my face, and now it's out there pretending to be me, killing people.'

Gran sighed again but said nothing.

'You believe me!' Callum gasped.

'Yes, I do.'

195

'Why, Gran? You're not superstitious! You don't even go to church! So why do you believe me?'

'Callum,' Gran said, her voice still quiet and even. 'We need to talk. There's a lot you don't know that I suppose I have to tell you. Things about me, and about yourself. And –'

She paused, then added reluctantly, 'And about your father.'

Chapter 19

'Your father was a chime child,' Gran said. 'Do you know what a chime child is?'

'Someone born beneath a full moon between midnight on Friday and cockcrow on Saturday,' replied Callum. 'Born with the ability to see ghosts.'

Gran nodded. 'You're a chime child too,' she said. 'I'm not – not really. I was born at the cusp of the chime hours, after sunrise, so my powers were limited.'

'You have powers?' Callum cried incredulously. 'You can see ghosts too?'

'No.' Gran shook her head. 'The powers of even the strongest chime children fade at eighteen. I've had to work at what I can do. I've learned some tricks, mostly charms and wards – I suppose you'd call it magic.' She coughed nervously. 'I'm surprised you haven't noticed. I've grown a bit careless with the radio.'

'You're always telling it to shut up, and it does! You told me it was the frequency cutting out!' Callum stared, wide-eyed. 'Gran, you hypocrite!' he said angrily. 'You called Melissa a witch, just because of the clothes she wears, and then you turn around and have a chat with your enchanted radio?'

'Yes, well, I was impatient with Melissa,' Gran admitted, her tone defensive. 'But I don't want witches here, or potential witches. Almost everything I do is designed to cut down on free-floating magic, to keep it out, to make things *normal*. You don't like it, do you, seeing ghosts? I've done this for you, Callum. I –'

Gran stood up suddenly. She sounded less sure of herself now.

'Thirteen years ago, your father disappeared. Peter was my son, my only child. I tell people he "just walked out" because that's what people say when a man abandons his young wife. But the truth is a bit more dramatic than that. The truth is, he vanished.'

Callum listened in silence. There was nothing he could say.

'It's still an open file with the police,' Gran continued. 'He could have killed himself, he could have been kidnapped by drug smugglers or something. I suppose he could have run away to Morocco with some new girlfriend. No one knows what happened to him.'

'What about his friends?' Callum asked. 'Didn't they know anything?'

'He didn't have many friends,' Gran said. 'Peter wasn't an easy person to get to know. When he first started going out with your mum, she and I used to have a good laugh about it behind his back. "Has he asked you to marry him yet?" I'd say, and she'd smile mysteriously and answer, "He's thinking about it. Still waters run deep." Even as a child he kept himself to himself. He was independent, unsentimental. A bit like you in some ways.'

'Like *you*,' Callum replied.

Gran smiled shortly. 'Yes, I suppose so. When Peter disappeared, your mother and I were both miserable, and it drew us together. Neither of us had any family nearby. Helen moved in here with me for some while – she knew she wouldn't get any sympathy from her parents in Cornwall, who'd told her a million times that her relationship with Peter would never work. She and I waited together, both of us hoping and hoping for a lead. Nothing turned up. And then she realised she was pregnant.'

'With me,' Callum breathed. 'But Dad didn't know?'

Gran shook her head.

Callum was silent. He felt as though some part of him had been cut off.

My dad never even knew about me.

He could tell it pained Gran, too.

'Callum, I'm sorry. There are a lot of reasons I haven't told you any of this. That's one of them.'

'Just get it over with,' Callum said. 'Or isn't there any more? He disappeared, the police couldn't find him, and I was born a few months later?'

Gran nodded. 'That's pretty much what happened. That's all your mother knew about it. But I had other ideas.'

She began to pace. The sitting room seemed suddenly too small to contain her.

'I thought all along that there was another possibility besides all the guesses the police were making. Your father was like you – he saw ghosts and monsters. Even after he grew out of his chime powers, he used to travel the country, looking for demons, hoping to fight them.' Gran shook her head. 'I think, in the end, one of them might have killed him. I knew you were a chime child too, and I couldn't bear the idea that I might lose you like that as well. So I began to weave a web of protection around you –'

'Of magic?' Callum interrupted.

Gran nodded. 'It was easy, at first, because Helen stayed with me for two years and you were always under my eye. So I started with the house. The rowan tree was already growing by the door and I had the garden wall reinforced with iron rails.'

Melissa's voice echoed in Callum's memory.

Iron keeps away the fairies . . . Rowan works against witches . . .

'I filled the flower beds with sympathetic herbs,

201

planted holly beneath the windows. I wove folk remedies into a charmed barrier around the cottage. I got better at it as I went along. I *liked* doing it, you know; there's a certain artistry, a satisfying creativity, to making any kind of orderly pattern. I'm quite proud of it, really.'

'What happened when Mum moved into our flat in the town?'

'Some of the spells I made worked on you directly. And I added some charms over your mum's window boxes and around the building there in town. The spells aren't just protective; they're concealing. I wanted to *hide* you. So your powers have been hidden, not just from whatever's out there, but also from yourself.'

Callum was still listening quietly, growing increasingly annoyed with Gran's pacing. Then he realised that it wasn't the pacing that was making him angry: it was what she was saying. He didn't blame his grandmother for trying to protect him. But to do it without his knowledge, to use some sort of magic on him without telling him what was going on, that felt like betrayal.

'After your mother died and you moved in with me, I stepped up the security. Once you're inside this house, nothing should be able to find you. You're safe.'

Gran finally stood still. She rested her hands on her hips and looked at Callum.

'Safe?' Callum blurted angrily. 'Safe? I'm seeing more ghosts than ever. I can predict the future. The thing with no face – or with *my* face, depending on its dress sense – that thing is killing my schoolmates. I think your spells are collapsing.'

'I don't think it's the strength of my spells that's letting you down,' Gran said with sorrow in her voice. 'Quite the opposite. Your own powers are getting stronger. You're getting older, Callum. You've become more difficult to hide. I thought that if I kept you away from the occult – brought you up to believe it was all stuff-and-nonsense – then maybe those powers wouldn't be triggered.'

'All you did was make me feel like a lunatic!' Callum exclaimed in outrage. 'You made me think I was the only person like this in the world!'

'It was a gamble,' Gran said, her hands out towards

Callum. 'I thought it might work. Sometimes a chime child doesn't know his or her own strengths. I tried to keep your power hidden as best I could. I tried, but obviously I failed. I'm sorry.'

Gran leaned heavily against the back of her armchair. She looked old and tired, but Callum didn't have it in him to feel sorry for her. He could not believe how much she had been hiding from him. He felt anger burning up inside him, like a volcano.

'Well, maybe I can tell you what happened to my father,' Callum raged. 'Maybe this thing without a face tore out his eyes and ate them!'

'His body was never found,' Gran said wearily. 'Your monster leaves bodies behind, doesn't it?'

'Did he even know he was a chime child, or did you hide that from him, too? What else are you hiding from me?'

'Oh, Callum.' Gran shook her head. 'Part of the reason I felt so strongly about protecting you is because I failed to protect your father. Yes, he knew he was a chime child. He was so sure of his abilities, and so quick and able when he used them. There's a set of books he studied – books passed down from one generation of chime children to the next, containing information about the Netherworld –'

'Books,' Callum repeated, as evenly as he could. 'I'm guessing these would be the books on that hidden shelf up there, then? The ones you're so precious about, you threw my friend out of the house when she went near them? Passed from one generation to the next. So they should be *mine*.'

If Gran was surprised to learn that he knew about the secret library, she didn't show it.

'I'm sorry, Callum,' she said again, with that same weary air of defeat. 'I was wrong.'

'Wrong? No kidding!' Callum yelled. 'You've tried to hide me, but that monster – whatever it is – still found me, didn't it? It stood on the patio, grinning at me last night. It chased me halfway around the school today. It knows I'm here. All it has to do is wait!'

Now Callum was on his feet, too. He faced his grandmother. 'You didn't want to trigger my powers? I'm being blown off the map by them, and I don't know *anything* about them! What is this thing that's

205

after me? What does it want? What does it *do* – besides rip out people's eyes? Why does it do that? How can it be stopped? Are you hiding that from me as well?'

'No, Callum, I'm not. I don't know how to stop it.'

'At least tell me what it is! You say you've been trying to protect me all my life – now's your chance to really do it. Tell me!'

'Callum, I don't *know* what it is.' Gran's voice was so despairing that Callum knew she was telling the truth. 'But I'll tell you what. We don't need to stay here. If the Shadowing is beginning, we can leave. We –'

Gran broke off, clapping a hand to her mouth. Callum stared at her. A horrible twisting sensation in his stomach told him that they had reached the deepest secret of all.

'What's the Shadowing, Gran?'

'It's nothing,' replied Gran, hastily. 'But I'm serious, Callum. We can pack a couple of rucksacks in ten minutes. We've still got time to catch a train to Manchester tonight. We could be in the Lake District in a couple of hours. We can lie low for the weekend and make plans. Figure out our next move. I've got a friend from school who lives in Scotland –'

'Gran. Gran!' Callum interrupted. 'This isn't helpful. What do you mean "if the Shadowing is beginning"?'

'Don't ask me, Callum.' Gran's voice was desperate. 'I can't tell you.'

'You have to!'

'Callum, I can't!' snapped Gran. 'It's too dangerous. I know this is hard, but you just have to trust me.'

Callum shook his head. Maybe Gran could keep him safe, and maybe she couldn't. Either way, he was fed up with being lied to.

'If you won't give me answers, I'll have to get them some other way.'

Yanking open the door, Callum stormed out of the cottage. He stomped up the path to the front gate, shoulders hunched and head down, gritting his teeth as he tensed himself for the harrowing walk through Marlock Wood.

'Callum, come back!' Gran called after him in desperation. 'It's not safe!'

Callum didn't answer.

He set off up the road into the dark.

Chapter 20

Halfway through Marlock Wood, Callum began to run. His heels hit the road with dull thumps. He was running the race of his nightmare again, driven by dread, not knowing where he'd end up. But in the nightmare, his surroundings had been unfamiliar. Now he knew where he was. Now he was awake. He didn't know if he was running towards the menace of his evil dream or away from it, but he knew it was real.

He ran out of the wood and through the tidy, empty streets of the housing estate, cars and garden walls lit faintly orange by the street lights. When he reached

Marlock High Street at the top of the hill, Callum paused. He had lost all sense of time waiting in the police station, and he had no idea how late it was now. The high street, usually quite lively on a Friday night as its pubs and restaurants began their weekend rush, was deserted by the living. Maybe news of Ed's murder had spread and was keeping people off the streets. Only the fluttering, pale ghosts came and went along the pavements. Callum ignored them. It seemed strange that these harmless shades had once seemed so frightening. Compared to what was hunting him now, they were no danger.

Panting a little as he looked around, Callum saw the sign that pointed towards the train station. The yellow-brick house by the station, Melissa had said. That was where she lived – the only place he might find the answers he needed. He hoped it wasn't too late to make an unexpected visit. At the station approach he glanced up at the dial on the nineteenth-century clock tower and was surprised to see that it wasn't yet nine o'clock.

Melissa's house was small and smart, with a brass

plate on the door that said 'Old Stationmaster's Cottage'. Callum waited until he was breathing normally before he rang the bell.

Melissa answered the door herself. She opened her mouth to exclaim aloud, then clapped both hands over it before any sound came out. For a moment Callum thought she was going to hug him, and he stepped back warily. But she managed to restrain herself. Instead, she grabbed his arm with one hand and hauled him inside, holding a finger to her lips with the other hand to warn Callum not to say anything. Then she called out over her shoulder, 'It's one of my friends from school, Mum. Everybody's so upset about what happened today. Can I make him a cup of tea?'

'Right-o,' called a woman's voice from the front room. 'Come in and have a chat then, if you like. Best to talk about it.'

'Thanks, Mum.'

'And try not to make a *mess*, Melissa.'

Melissa screwed up her face and led Callum to the kitchen.

Her house seemed enormous to him. It wasn't really much more than a cottage itself, but the ceilings were higher and it was three times as wide as the Nether Marlock alms houses. The kitchen had been extended with a modern glassed-in area to make room for an ageing sofa and large pine table stacked with magazines and newspapers.

'I'm so glad to see you,' Melissa said with honest warmth, briskly clicking the switch on the electric kettle and banging down two mugs on the crowded table. 'But look, I'm not going to take you in to talk to my mum. Everyone in town's gone hysterical over this murder and she's not too happy about me being called as a witness. What happened? Did they prove your alibi?'

Callum nodded.

'Yes!' Melissa crowed, slapping one palm down on the tabletop hard enough to make the mugs jump. 'I'm so pleased! So does that mean you're free?'

'Depends on your definition of freedom,' Callum said, leaning his elbows on the table and burying his face in his hands. After a moment he ran his fingers through his hair – it was tangled as a bird's nest after this evening's carry-on. He looked up at Melissa. 'I think I know what's happening,' he said.

Over mugs of stewed tea that neither of them could drink, Callum told Melissa everything that had happened over the past week. He left out nothing, not even the details of his dream, his meeting with Jacob, or the fights with his grandmother. Even Melissa, who had been so eager to believe that Callum was a chime child, looked overwhelmed by the undeniable connection of the faceless monster with Ed's murder – and with Callum himself.

She bit her lip, then stood up, went to the back door, and looked out into the night.

'Come on,' she said, and beckoned. 'The best thing you can do – the *only* thing you can do – is to find this Jacob. OK, you don't know what he is, but he's obviously not the one who's killing kids. You said yourself he's a ghost, not a monster like this other thing. Maybe he knows what's going on. He might have answers.'

'He tried to warn me,' Callum said, thinking. 'But I

thought he was threatening me. I thought it *was* him doing the killing. You're right. I don't know if he can be trusted, but . . .'

But whatever else Jacob might be hiding, his warning about the 'dark reflection' had been accurate. And now that Callum thought about it, even Doom's howling had only ever served to protect him. It had scared him, true, but it had also scared off Ed and his gang, and even the faceless thing that was trying to kill him.

'I don't know if any ghost can be trusted,' Callum said. 'But no ghost has ever hurt me, and Jacob's the only one who's ever tried to talk to me. Maybe he *does* have answers.'

'Come on, then,' said Melissa. 'He hangs out in the churchyard, right? So we need to go there. If we sneak out by the back door, I don't need to tell my mum we're going. I'll leave a note, though.' She scribbled a brief excuse on a pad and stuck it on the fridge. 'Hopefully she won't see it till I get back.'

'Aren't you afraid?' Callum marvelled.

'Of what? "Ancient monuments can be dangerous"?'

Melissa gave a hollow laugh, but then her face became serious. 'Well, I guess I am. Aren't you?' She opened the back door softly. 'I'm not afraid of walking through the woods; not usually anyway, so that's all I'm thinking about at the moment. If I sit here moping about Ed I'll just get myself down. At least your faceless monster isn't going after *my* eyes.'

'You don't know that,' Callum said. 'Don't even think it.'

'I told you, I'm only thinking about getting myself out the door. Now just come on, before I change my mind!'

Callum followed Melissa. They made their way cautiously down the side path to the front of the house. Melissa gave the air a little victorious punch when they got through the front gate without being noticed. Callum answered her with a grim smile under the street lamp.

'Come on, then. Let's get this over with.'

*

The moon was rising over Marlock Wood as they came to the lane that led to the ruined church. Now Melissa let Callum lead her.

'Do you think your Grim will be there, too?' she asked in a low voice, sounding strangely eager. 'Do you think I'll be able to see it?'

'I don't know.' The moonlight cast blue shadows over the old tombstones. 'Be careful where you walk,' Callum added, as though the ordinary danger of uneven ground was all they had to worry about. His voice sounded hollow as he spoke.

They picked their way through the overgrown graves until they came to the church.

'It was round here that I saw him,' whispered Callum. 'Are you sure you want to do this?'

Melissa nodded, swallowing hard. Callum gave her a tight smile and they stepped round the corner of the church.

Jacob was standing by the ancient yew tree, bathed in the moonlight. The gigantic black Grim, Doom, sat on his haunches at Jacob's heel. They looked as if they'd been waiting there ever since the day the

Victorian photographer had tried to capture their image with collodion and silver nitrate. As Jacob caught sight of Callum, the faintest trace of a smile played on his lips, but when Melissa stepped into view he frowned.

'She is a mortal,' said Jacob accusingly.

'So am I,' Callum answered fiercely.

'You know well what I mean. She's not a chime child. She has no connection to the Netherworld. She should not be here.'

'Why not?' Callum stood his ground. 'She lives in Marlock too. Maybe her ancestors are buried in this churchyard.'

Melissa moved closer to Callum's side.

'Are you talking to *him* – to the ghost? Is he here now?' She drew a sharp breath. 'Can you see the Grim?'

Callum gave a curt nod. 'Jacob's unhappy that you're here,' he said softly. 'Don't worry. I'm going to insist.' He turned back to Jacob.

'Melissa's a translator,' Callum told him. 'She's not of your world, but she understands it. More than that – she's fluent in it. I can see things she can't, but I don't know what they are. Melissa knows their names. She knows how things work. She's told me more than you have, and more clearly. She can help.'

Jacob paused, and looked Melissa up and down suspiciously. After a moment he said with disdain, 'Will she scream and run if she sees me?'

Callum carefully repeated the question, to warn Melissa. 'Will you scream and run from Jacob?'

Melissa gave a snort. 'Would I be here if I was going to scream and run? I – *Oh*.'

Jacob tilted his head towards Callum with a wry smile.

'She can see me now.'

'Is the Grim yours?' Melissa asked softly, and it took Callum a stunned moment to realise that she was addressing the question directly to Jacob without showing any further surprise or fear. The great black dog stared back at Melissa, its eyes glowing like red-hot coals in the darkness.

'Doom goes with me where I go,' Jacob answered briefly. 'I do not own him. Come with me into the church and we can talk. You are not safe, walking abroad in this wood, either by daylight or in moonlight. Come inside.'

Doom suddenly loped forward. Callum couldn't help but flinch as the gigantic hound passed them in a rush of icy wind. Melissa took a firm grip on Callum's elbow, and they passed through the doorway of the ruined church together, Jacob following behind.

The floor of the roofless building was a tangle of weeds and nettles. A narrow path wound towards the gaping black hole of a doorway that led to the tower stairs. Doom stopped halfway along this path and turned around. Jacob joined him.

'This is no longer a true sanctuary,' Jacob said, 'but as long as the moonlight falls on the altar steps, it holds a memory of its sacred past, and evil spirits will think twice before they enter here.'

Jacob's depthless eyes pinned Callum with a piercing stare. 'I know you think I am likely evil too. When last we met, you banished me from your home and accused me of murder. So tell me – what has brought you back to us so fearlessly now?'

Callum threw open his hands in frustration. Wasn't it obvious?

'The dark reflection.'

Doom growled, low in his throat, like the distant rumble of thunder. Jacob laid a gleaming white hand on the huge dog's black head.

'You have seen it?' Jacob asked seriously.

'It killed a boy at our school.'

'Have you *seen* it?' Jacob insisted.

'It came into the garden last night,' Callum said in a hushed voice. 'It had no face, but then it took *my* face. What is it?'

'It is a Fetch,' said Jacob. 'A demon from the Netherworld. And it has crossed into the world of daylight with bold impudence. It is a fearsome hunter, a tracker without parallel.'

'A Fetch!' Melissa cried. 'Of course – how stupid of me! "The dark reflection"!'

'You know it?' Jacob asked in surprise.

'I know of it,' Melissa answered. 'I should have recognised it when Callum talked about it at my house earlier. But I was still so shocked about Ed, and worried about Callum being accused of murder, I just didn't make the connection. Some translator I am! I know exactly what you're talking about. They call a Fetch "the dark reflection" because it doesn't have a face of its own, so if it wants to pass for a human it has to take on someone else's face and form. It can't even make up its own idea of a face – it has to use the face of someone it's seen before. And . . .'

She turned to Callum in excited triumph.

'It has a weakness!' she exclaimed. 'You can catch a Fetch off guard by showing it its own true reflection: it *hates* to look at its unmasked skin.' Melissa shivered, and hopped from foot to foot a couple of times. It was growing colder. 'It's in my book, that dictionary I showed you.'

Jacob nodded, his hand still buried in Doom's dark fur. 'You are quite some translator,' he said. 'A human girl who can tell the Fetch's weakness? A rare thing indeed.'

'The Fetch ate . . .' Callum swallowed and tried again. 'The boy it killed, it ate his eyes. Why does it do that?'

Jacob's mouth narrowed with distaste.

'The eyes of its victims give the Fetch its power,' he explained. 'But there is another reason too. Some people believe that, after death, the eyes of a murder victim hold an image of the true face of their killer, seeing them for what they really are. It is an old myth, but I think there is some truth to it. The Fetch blinds its victims so that it does not have to look at its own reflection in their dead eyes.'

Callum couldn't repress a shudder.

'But why is it here?'

Jacob bowed his head. 'It is hunting the chime children. There have never been many of our kind. Now there are fewer still. You may be the last chime child, Callum – the last living.'

Callum shook his head.

'What does that mean?'

'It means that now the Fetch is hunting you alone. You are its final victim. It will not rest until it has tracked you down and satisfied its hunger with your eyes.'

Chapter 21

The easy catch outside the school has whetted the Hunter's appetite. It has never felt more alert: its senses at their peak, its awareness of the real quarry electrifying. It knows where the boy is, knows exactly where to find him.

The Hunter tracks silently through the trees towards the abandoned church. The trail is clear and sharp. The Hunter does not need moonlight to find the way, but it enjoys the blue glow that will illuminate the terror on the boy's face when he is finally caught. The game has gone on long enough.

The Hunter arrives at the church. But the quarry is not alone. There is a mortal girl there too. She is no matter, but there are other, more potent, beings as well: creatures of the Netherworld, an unusual ghost and a spirit hound. The ghost is speaking to the mortal children as if they share the same world.

The Hunter would rather not let these others watch it feed — a ghost will not scream and flee in terror of the Hunter as a living being will, and a Churchyard Grim is a formidable opponent. The Hunter does not fear such things; it does not understand fear, though it is amusing to see it in mortals. Still, for now the Hunter is outnumbered. Very likely it will not be able to take its prey by surprise here. The boy must be lured to his own, carefully guarded dwelling place, where the ghosts cannot enter.

The Hunter knows how it can cross that charmed threshold. It only needs an invitation. And it is already masked with the boy's own face.

The Hunter smiles with its borrowed mouth. It passes by the church without any further hesitation.

It heads towards the lighted cottage.

Chapter 22

Doom growled.

It was the same sound the great dog had made when Jacob first mentioned the Fetch, beginning low in the hound's deep chest and rising to a dull roar. Then Doom spun round and snapped his long, white fangs. He took a few steps towards the western end of the church, where the dark tower squatted, and stopped, sniffing the air. The growl rose again in the beast's throat as he gazed piercingly at the church wall, as though he could see or sense something beyond it.

'Doom,' Jacob said in his echoing voice, and the dog turned a querying head to look at his master. 'Let. Sit.

These mortal beings are safe enough here for the moment.'

Doom whined. It, too, was a fearful sound, like the wail of a man being tortured. Melissa covered her ears.

'Quiet, Doom,' Jacob ordered. 'Guard the door, if you must. I have urgent business with the chime child.'

Doom slunk to the door in a rush of shadows and spread his enormous body at full length across the ruined threshold of the church. Callum felt increasingly trapped; not only was he surrounded by the church's stone walls, but the entry was blocked by the waiting Grim.

Jacob's bloodless lips quirked suddenly into his faint, wry smile.

'You still fear we mean you harm.' It wasn't a question.

Callum took a deep breath. 'You've agreed to trust Melissa. I've agreed to trust you. We're even.'

Jacob nodded. 'Good. Let me tell you what I am.'

'We're listening.'

The pale ghost looked away. He stood casually, with

his gleaming white hands hidden in the invisible pockets of his trousers. His unwillingness to face Callum and Melissa as he spoke gave Jacob an air of embarrassment, as if he was sharing a shameful secret.

'I said that you may be the last living chime child,' he said slowly. 'But there are others. Others like me. I too came into this world in the chime hours, but not as one of the living. I was stillborn, dead at the moment of my birth. I am the ghost of a child who never lived, born more than a hundred years ago. I am one of the Born Dead.'

Jacob's shoulders rose and fell in a silent sigh. 'Because I never drew breath, I was buried unbaptised, in the unconsecrated plot beyond the yew tree. But my mother named me Jacob. My name is all she gave me.'

'But if you're the ghost of a baby, how come you look like you're our age?' asked Callum.

'The Born Dead are given the power to choose their shape,' explained Jacob. 'I chose this – the form of the boy I would have grown into had I lived.'

'You're bleeding,' Melissa interrupted faintly.

A line of black blood trickled, glistening, down Jacob's throat. The ghost frowned, and swiped the blood on to his fingers.

'It doesn't matter,' he said. 'I can't control it. An echo of my birth, perhaps . . .'

Melissa and Callum exchanged horrified glances in the dim light. Jacob held up his hand and the blood slowly faded away.

'So what does it mean to be one of the Born Dead?' asked Melissa. 'I've never heard of you before.'

'We haunt the boundaries between the Netherworld and the realm of the living, belonging neither in one world nor the other. It is a lonely business. When I first found myself to be a waking spirit, I raised this dog's shade from its grave to be my companion.' Jacob cast a glance at Doom, crouched by the church door. The great beast seemed unaware his master was talking about him. 'It caused a deal of upset in the village. No one even knew Nether Marlock *had* a Church Grim before I summoned the dog's spirit. But I needed a companion. And a Grim is a formidable foe against the demons of the Netherworld. Doom is my protector, as he protects all the humans buried in this churchyard; and he will protect you, too, if I command it.'

'But what does this have to do with the Fetch?' Callum asked.

Jacob turned to look at Callum and Melissa directly. Then he held out his long white hands, palms facing upwards.

'Touch me,' Jacob commanded.

Callum and Melissa glanced at each other in alarm.

'Can we?' Melissa said. 'If you're a ghost, we shouldn't be able to, right?'

Jacob nodded.

'Well, there you are,' she said without conviction.

'Try.'

Melissa raised her hand tentatively. Then she reached toward Jacob's palm and laid her hand against it.

'Oh!'

She jumped as though she'd received a jolt of electricity through her whole body, but she kept her palm held steadily against Jacob's.

'Should that happen?' Melissa whispered.

Jacob looked at Callum, the tilt of his head challenging. He shook the long, black hair out of his face.

'Go on.'

Callum laid his living hand against the ghost's dead palm.

It was cold. But Callum could feel it, the shape of it – dry, lifeless skin without any heat of its own. It wasn't a repellent touch, not clammy or icy, just lifeless, like a handful of dead leaves.

'How?' Callum croaked. 'I've never been able to touch a ghost. How are we able to touch you?'

'Once in a century, this happens.' Jacob spoke quietly, but his bell-like voice was no less commanding. 'Once every century, for thirteen months – a year by the moon's clock – comes a time called the Shadowing.'

Callum's heart skipped a beat. 'The Shadowing . . .'

'You have heard the word before?' Jacob's expression was surprised.

'Not till tonight. My gran mentioned it, but she wouldn't tell me what it meant. She said it was dangerous.'

Jacob nodded. 'It is. More dangerous than you can possibly imagine. While the Shadowing lasts, the boundaries of your mortal world and the Netherworld are weakened.'

'The Netherworld – the world of the dead?' Melissa asked.

'Some of the dead dwell in the Netherworld,' Jacob answered. 'But they are not its only inhabitants. The Netherworld exists alongside the mortal world; its creatures unseen and invisible to mortal eyes. Not just the spirits of the dead, but also beings of magic and evil. Demons. Monsters. When the boundaries between the worlds are weak, the beings of the Netherworld can cross the border between the worlds and enter the realm you know.'

'And we can touch,' Melissa said in wonder.

Jacob nodded. 'The Shadowing is not upon us yet, but it is close, and as I am a boundary-dweller, it is already affecting me – just as it has been affecting you, Callum.'

'What does it have to do with me?' said Callum.

'Your powers have been given to you for a reason,'

replied Jacob. 'The power to see the dead, to sense evil, to resist magic. You are a warrior, Callum. You and every other chime child. You are the guardians of the boundary. It is your fate to protect this mortal world from the dark forces that threaten it.'

Callum closed his eyes, blotting out Melissa's amazed expression. *A warrior? How could he be a warrior?*

'But you said this happens every century, the Shadowing,' he said in a low voice. 'What's so different about *this* time?'

'This time,' Jacob said, his voice suddenly fierce, 'there is a conspiracy. A plot between the demon powers of the Netherworld and the evil-doers of this. The Shadowing has not yet begun – the Fetch could not have crossed into the mortal realm without help from this side. And why is it only killing chime children? A Fetch can take any child, any human, and yet this one is picking and choosing its prey. It is no glutton – it is a gourmet. An assassin. I think the chime children are being singled out for destruction.'

'And they're being killed just before the Shadowing begins – just when their protection is most needed,'

Melissa said, understanding flooding her eyes.

Callum dropped his hand from Jacob's palm.

'And why do you care?'

Jacob shrugged. 'I have no wish to exist in a world dominated by evil, any more than you do. My existence is lonely enough as it is.' Jacob's pale lips formed the faint, sad smile that made him seem more human.

Callum turned to look at the great shadow of Doom lying in the doorway.

'You said that Doom protects you.'

'Yes. And could protect you, too, if you would accept my help. Together, perhaps, we can defeat the Fetch that stalks you.' Jacob glanced at Melissa, who still held her palm stalwartly against Jacob's hand.

'I'll help too,' she said.

Jacob nodded. 'Translator.'

Suddenly angry, Callum glared at Jacob and Melissa. They seemed to have formed a united front, ready to decide his destiny for him. Rage swelled up in his chest.

'Why is this my fight?' Callum demanded. 'I didn't ask for this. I hate these so-called chime child powers,

I've always hated them. Why should I use them for anything?'

'Callum!' Melissa swung around to face him in surprise.

'I mean it. Why am I responsible? I just want to be normal. It's all I've ever wanted.'

'But you aren't normal, Callum,' retorted Melissa. 'You're special. You have a gift –'

Callum snorted. 'Some gift. The chance to wage a one-man war against the Netherworld. No thanks.'

Melissa put her hands on her hips. 'You said you wanted to know what was happening and now you do. The Fetch is here to kill the chime children – all of them. That includes you. Isn't saving yourself a good enough reason?'

At the very moment Melissa spoke the word 'yourself', Callum's fingers went numb.

He shook his hands in panic, but already the burning pins-and-needles sensation was spreading through his fingertips as though he'd shoved them in a patch of nettles. It was the strongest warning of a premonition that he'd ever had, and the most painful. Then another vision hit him like a block of falling masonry.

It was the Fetch. For one second, he saw the demon in its true form, a stick figure with no skin and no shadow. Then the vision flickered and he saw it in its present shape – his own body. Even though he had never seen himself walking, he could tell that in its disguise the Fetch was his identical twin. It strode through the tangled trees of Marlock Wood with its shoulders hunched, as Callum always did when he walked along the old road, avoiding looking up from his feet for fear of seeing the ghosts that haunted the lane.

This is what I look like.

The furtive, youthful figure cast a faint shadow in the bright moonlight, and Callum realised with a sudden jolt that the moonlight he saw in his head, shining down on the figure of the Fetch as it paced through Marlock Wood, was the same moonlight that shone through the roofless ruin of the church. The same moonlight that bathed him now.

Now. It was happening now. The Fetch was on the

road through the woods. And it was heading downhill. Not towards the church, not towards Callum, but towards another destination altogether.

It was heading for the row of ruined alms cottages.

In Callum's mind, he saw the figure stop outside the low brick wall and leap over the wooden gate, just as Callum himself had done so many times that week.

The light was on over the porch. The curtains were open. Gran was inside, waiting for Callum to come home. The Fetch walked up the path to the door of the cottage, wearing Callum's own embarrassed smile of apology, and with a hand identical to his own, lifted the brass knocker.

Chapter 23

Gran sat wearily in her favourite chair in the nook under the stairs, from which she could see a long way up the road. Cadbury was prowling restlessly, but when she got up to let him out, the cat hissed and backed away from the door. She stood staring up the empty road for a minute before she shut the door again, biting her lip. After a moment, she locked it.

'Where is he?' Gran muttered. Cadbury stopped his prowling and sat down on his haunches to look at her. 'What do I do, Cadbury? It's not safe for him to be out there alone. But if I go off to try and find him and he comes back . . .'

Gran wrung her hands together in indecision. 'What do I *do?*' she repeated.

Cadbury jumped up to sit on top of the bulky old cassette player. It immediately began to play one of Gran's favourite big-band tunes.

'Thanks,' Gran sighed. 'I guess you're right. I've small hope of finding him, and no hope of protecting him outside these walls. We'll just have to wait it out and hope for the best. But he's so angry. And that's my fault; my fault for deceiving him. No wonder he was confused and upset.'

She felt old and tired, but she couldn't sit down again. She'd made herself a cup of tea earlier, but it had gone stone cold and she hadn't touched it.

'Come on, Cadbury,' she said. 'Let's switch on every light in the house. Let's make this place into a beacon.'

She had been in two minds about turning on the lights – she could see the road better with the lights in the sitting room off – but she needed something practical to do. She knew that Callum looked for the light when he made his way back through the wood, and she wanted him to feel welcome.

Walking upstairs, she switched on the overhead lights in both bedrooms, the bedside lamps, and the landing light. With the upstairs windows of the cottage ablaze, Gran came back down and turned on all the other lights.

The boy had been gone for over an hour now. Where? It was unlikely Callum had gone to meet anyone he knew from school, unless it was the girl, Melissa. Despite her initial reaction when she'd found the girl nosing through the books, Gran had had to change her opinion of Melissa that afternoon. She had stood at the door, insistently rapping the brass knocker with the urgency of a fire alarm and calling wildly. Gran had been in the back garden, trying to figure out why the row of cabbages by the wall had gone black and mouldy overnight. She hadn't heard the phone when Callum had been given his one call. But there had been no way to miss Melissa's shouting. It carried over the roof of the little cottage.

Mrs Scott! Mrs Scott! Callum's in trouble!

Why, Melissa had even been ahead of the *police*! They had met the patrol car coming down the road through Marlock Wood as they were walking back up to town together. *A right bright spark*, the sergeant had called her.

So maybe Callum had gone to see Melissa. That would make sense. The Old Stationmaster's Cottage, that was where Callum had said she lived. A pleasant enough place, the yellow bricks in good repair, and nice flowers in the window boxes.

But the yellow-brick house wasn't *safe* – it wasn't protected by a web of charms, and its ordinary walls would be no protection against the invasion of a monster from the Netherworld that even she didn't recognise.

'Oh, *why* doesn't he come home!' Gran exclaimed, going to the window again.

She pressed her face against the cold glass and cupped her hands around her eyes, trying to see beyond the reflection of light and firelight from the room behind her. The moon was out and high now – it was a beautiful clear evening. Gran couldn't see anyone on the road. She sighed and went into the kitchen to put the kettle on. Callum might want a hot drink when he came back. And she could do with a fresh cup of tea.

The kettle had just reached the boil when Gran heard the sound of the brass knocker, Callum's signature firm drumming.

Thank God!

She was at the door in three strides, in less than a second.

'Callum!' she cried out. 'Thank goodness, I've been so worried!'

Gran lifted the latch effortlessly – she couldn't figure out why Callum always had to fight such a battle with the old thing – and threw open the door.

The boy stood just off the doorstep, his untidy hair in his eyes. He looked hangdog and embarrassed, as though he was feeling a little ashamed of himself. He'd either taken a step backwards waiting for her to open the door, or he'd had to lean across the porch to knock.

Cadbury let out a hiss, and backed away from the door with a tail the size of a chimney brush, then fled upstairs. The radio, too, gave a howl of static and went silent.

'Good grief, but that cat's wound up this evening! Callum, I'm so relieved you've come back.'

Gran pushed the door wide open and stepped aside so that Callum could come past her. But he just stood there, silently, on the other side of the doorstep looking at her with shy, beseeching eyes.

'I'm *so* sorry you had to find out the way you did, I really am, Callum. I've been going out of my mind myself all evening!'

Callum shrugged, and gave that characteristic shake of his head to get the hair out of his eyes, just as Peter had always done at that age. She felt such a surge of love for him that for a moment she couldn't speak. Then she found her voice again.

'Well, come in, for goodness sake! Don't stand out there in the shadows! Come in!'

Callum smiled. At her invitation, he stepped across her threshold, came into the house and closed the door behind him.

Chapter 24

Callum leaped over the back of Doom as if he was vaulting a stone wall. The cold air surrounding the great Grim's body clawed at his legs like wind off a frozen canal, and then he was out in the open.

The others followed almost as quickly. The rough ground of the old churchyard was treacherous underfoot. Callum tried to run and fell flat in two metres, cracking his elbow against the low iron railing surrounding the Victorian grave he'd tripped over.

Ancient monuments can be dangerous . . .

Seconds later Melissa stumbled on exactly the same railing. But Callum was on his feet again and didn't wait for her. He caught his jacket on the gate on the way out of the graveyard, ripped it free, and stumbled, cursing, down the lane to the road. Stark in his mind he remembered the image of the hand – *his own hand* – closing over the round brass knocker on Gran's green door and rapping at it firmly.

He didn't need a premonition to tell him what would happen next. Gran would open the door. She would think the Fetch was Callum. She would invite it in. And all the charms and magic in the world couldn't keep the Fetch from crossing Gran's threshold if she asked it in herself.

And then . . .

Callum sprinted down the lane, gasping for breath. What if he was too late, as he'd been again and again when the Fetch was ahead of him? Behind him he heard Melissa's running footsteps, and beyond that, the thud of Doom's paws on the road. He didn't look back to see how close they were, or whether Jacob was following too. His only thought was to get home.

Faster!

Reaching the cottage, Callum crashed through the

little garden gate and raced up the path.

'Callum, wait!'

It was Jacob's voice, but Callum didn't stop. He had no idea how to fight the Fetch, but he knew he had to stop it before . . .

With Melissa on his heels, Callum slammed into the door, twisting the old-fashioned latch upwards. The door flew open and they stumbled into the room.

Gran was standing in front of the fire, her hands on her hips, a worried frown drawing her brows together. She did not look frightened. She looked concerned and frustrated. She was looking earnestly at the boy who stood facing her – a boy only a little shorter than Gran herself, broad-shouldered, in an anorak with a ragged hem identical to the one Callum was wearing.

For a moment, Callum stood frozen in amazement. It truly was like looking into a mirror.

Beware the dark reflection.

And then Callum cried out, '*Gran!*'

The Fetch and Gran both turned at the same moment. Gran's eyes flew wide and her mouth dropped open in shock and understanding. Seeing

Callum standing in the same room as his doppelgänger, she knew at once what had happened.

Gran didn't hesitate. She stepped between the Fetch and Callum, holding her arms out to bar the monster's path.

'Callum, run!'

The Fetch reached out with Callum's arms. But the strength in those arms was far greater than Callum's own. In its rage, the Fetch's nails and teeth lengthened, so that suddenly it looked more like a demon than a boy; a parody of Callum, with claws like talons and teeth like the fangs of a prehistoric monster.

With one of these hideous claws it seized Gran by the shoulder, and with the other it grabbed her by the hair. Then it lifted her off her feet, her face frozen in a wide stare of astonishment and horror, and hurled her like a doll across the room. Her body crashed hard against the wall and she slid to the floor and lay still.

'Callum!' cried a voice.

Callum half turned. Jacob stood on the path, Doom crouched at his side, growling like a demonic tiger, showing teeth like sabres in the moonlight. Twin trails of black blood dripped like sweat down Jacob's temples and along his palms. The pair had kept pace with Callum on the road, but the barrier he had thrown up against the spectral boy and his dog still prevented either of them from moving even a fraction over Gran's doorstep.

'Quick,' cried Melissa. 'You have to invite them in!'

But the Fetch was too fast. Crossing the room in two quick strides, it slammed the door in the faces of the two ghosts. From beyond the solid wood, Doom let out a frenzied howl.

The Fetch stood for a moment, flexing its clawed talons, its alien features settling back into a face that looked like Callum's, although the fire did not leave its eyes, and in its twisted smile the teeth remained sharp and pointed.

Then it lunged forward with its hands spread, ready to grasp and tear.

Chapter 25

Focused only on Callum, the Fetch paid Melissa no attention. With all the strength in her body, she threw herself at Callum and pushed him out of the Fetch's path.

It was only a distraction – a brief one. The Fetch turned to follow Callum as he tumbled backwards. Melissa stepped sideways towards the hearth. Grabbing Gran's mug of cold tea, she hurled it at the back of the Fetch's head. The mug smashed against its skull, but Melissa might as well have hit the monster with a dandelion for all the notice it took.

'Rowan!' Callum cried, scrambling out of the way

on his hands and knees. 'Throw the rowan!'

Melissa seized the jar of hazel leaves and rowan berries from the table. Sensing she was about to attack with something more effective than cold tea, the Fetch turned to face her. Melissa hurled the jar at its head, but her aim was less accurate this time. The twigs and berries flew harmlessly past the Fetch's face and smashed at Callum's feet. He grabbed a slender twig of rowan as he got to his feet. It was the flimsiest weapon imaginable.

The Fetch stood still, its head tilted sideways, contemplating Callum. It was utterly unnerving to be stared at by his own face, seeing such burning hatred there.

The Fetch licked its lips and smiled. Then stepped forward again, claws raised.

Callum flourished the rowan, and the Fetch stopped, its burning eyes narrow.

Then it laughed, a hideous gurgling sound, as if its throat were being rubbed raw with sandpaper.

'Pitiful,' it said in a hoarse voice. 'Can this world do no better than you as its champion? A frightened child, cowering behind a handful of twigs?'

It *had* flinched, though. It had backed away from the touch of the rowan as though it feared it. Callum raised the twig higher, even though it felt like trying to meet a switchblade with a safety pin. If only he had a more substantial weapon.

That was it!

'Melissa!' Callum cried. 'The logs – they're rowan too!'

Melissa snatched up one of the stouter branches piled in the fire basket and tossed it to Callum. He dropped the twig and caught the branch.

The Fetch sneered.

'A sharpened lance might harm me, but not that stick. Fight with your hands, little boy, not with leaves and berries! Is the strength of your body mere illusion? Shall we test it?'

The Fetch leaped forward, its wicked talons slashing for Callum's throat. Callum fell back, lashing out, using the rowan branch as a cudgel to strike at the Fetch. The blow connected with the side of its head and the Fetch gave a snarl of pain.

The instant the charmed wood touched its skin, all illusion fell away. Callum's likeness vanished and the Fetch became itself once more, the skinless creature of vein and muscle that Callum had first seen in the garden. Its lipless teeth were clenched in fury, the naked cords of its throat tensed for attack. The wide, lidless eyes stared wrathfully at Callum.

With the speed of a striking viper, the Fetch seized Callum around the wrist. It moved so fast that Callum realised all the creature's earlier dodging and weaving had just been to lead him on. With a vicious wrench, the Fetch twisted Callum's arm until he was forced to let go of the branch, then brought its other hand flashing towards his head. Callum desperately flung his right hand out to block, but he couldn't get a grip on the slick surface of the Fetch's body. Almost carelessly, it tossed Callum across the room. He fell hard against the floor.

All the air was knocked out of Callum's lungs and he couldn't breathe. But blind instinct, his own reliable chime child Luck, made Callum roll aside as the Fetch's talons thrust at his face. A blade-like claw missed his eye by millimetres and scythed open a bloody gash in his skin from his cheekbone to his hairline. Callum gasped, clapping one hand to his torn face, and saw that behind the Fetch's back, Melissa had again taken advantage of being ignored long enough to seize the poker from the fireplace.

Callum shook his head desperately. He knew the Fetch was too strong for him – probably too strong for both of them together. Melissa's only hope was to avoid attracting attention.

Iron. Melissa mouthed. *It's iron.*

Of course – Callum remembered now that Gran's iron horseshoe and the rails that reinforced the brick wall were wards against the Netherworld.

The iron poker was not a sharpened lance, but it did have a hooked point for raking coals. As the Fetch loomed over Callum, ready for the kill, Melissa stepped up behind it and stabbed the hooked end into the back of the demon's neck with all the force she could muster.

The Fetch roared in fury, and whirled to meet Melissa, jerking the poker out of her hands. Reaching behind itself, it wrenched the poker free, sending a jet of clear fluid spurting from the wound in its neck. With one clawed hand, the monster seized Melissa by the throat, hauling her off her feet, raising the other to gouge at her eyes.

Still on the floor, gasping for breath and half-blinded by the stinging wound across his face, Callum's mind raced.

Didn't this creature have any weakness, even with a hole in its neck spurting whatever strange liquid ran in its veins instead of blood?

And then the answer struck him. Melissa had known it – that was what had impressed Jacob, the thing that had changed his mind about her and made him decide she might be a useful ally. She had known the Fetch's weakness – *its own reflection*.

Desperately, Callum scrambled towards the full-length curtains at the other side of the room.

'Hey!' Callum yelled. 'Hey! I'm the one you want to fight! I'm the last chime child! Let her go!'

The Fetch's dagger-like nails froze in front of Melissa's face. She clawed at the other taloned hand, the one that held her by the throat in its crushing grip, choking and sobbing for air, trying to twist her face away.

Callum could only count on having the Fetch's attention for one second. He didn't have time to open the curtains. Instead, he swung round and ripped them off the wall.

All the lights that Gran had turned on to guide Callum home were burning brightly – the fire, the lamps and the overhead ceiling light. With so much light focused against them, the full-length glass doors reflected the entire room. Their bright surface doubled the cottage as clearly as a mirror.

The Fetch, still holding Melissa by the throat, found itself face to face with its own reflection.

It stared, frozen, its eyes bulging.

Then its talons went lax and Melissa fell in a gasping heap on the floor at its feet.

Outside the cottage, Doom howled. The noise rose around the little house like a storm of screaming wind. Melissa cowered. The Fetch stumbled forwards, shaking its ghastly head, like a dreamer waking from a nightmare.

But it was too late. Callum was already behind it, hurling himself into a rugby tackle. His body slammed into the Fetch's knees, sending the monster flying. Almost in slow motion, Callum saw it reeling across the room towards the door. The glass shattered in a cascade of crystal shards, like an icy waterfall, as the Fetch fell through the door and out into the night.

Still barred from entering the house, Jacob stood in the garden, illuminated in the light flooding from the broken window. In his echoing voice, he rapped out a command that rang through the besieged cottage.

'Doom – destroy!'

*

The howling Grim wakes the Hunter from its trance.

It feels pain – the first time it has known the sensation for countless years. It does not remember staring at its reflection, but it knows it has been tricked. It has been thrust outside the cottage walls against its will. It spins with teeth bared – it can see the treacherous boy. It reaches, snarling, towards the broken threshold of the shattered glass door.

But the Grim hound is as fast as the Hunter. Unleashed, with eager and violent delight, the black dog leaps.

The Hunter goes down beneath the shadowy body like a bundle of sticks. It raises its claws to fight, but the Grim has it in its jaws, fangs sparkling in the silver moonlight, savaging and tearing as the Hunter struggles beneath it.

The Hunter makes no sound, but it knows it has met its match at last.

Despite the shining redness of its skinless face, its blood is clear as water. There is no gruesome gore to paint the ground, nor are the Grim's white teeth marred by any stain as it lowers its jaws to the Hunter's neck, and . . .

Darkness.

Chapter 26

Cold invaded the room.

Callum reached his unconscious grandmother first. Melissa was right behind him, hovering over his shoulder.

'Is she all right? Oh please tell me she's all right!'

There was a huge lump on the side of the old woman's head where she'd hit the wall, but to Callum's unspeakable relief, she was breathing steadily, and though her face was pale there was colour in her lips. Her skin was warm. Nothing seemed broken. Her pulse was steady.

'Help me,' Callum said. 'Move these chairs, get this glass out of the way . . .'

Melissa grabbed the shawls and cushions from the armchairs and spread them over the floor. Callum gently arranged his grandmother on her side in the recovery position. He was surprised at how light and fragile her body was when she was lying still – normally she seemed so strong and energetic.

'Are you OK?' he asked Melissa, turning his head to look at her.

'Yeah, just half strangled and scared brainless! But, Callum, your face!' Melissa pulled off one of her glittering scarves and began to mop blood from his cheek. 'Don't worry, this scarf only cost ninety pence at Shaman's . . .'

Callum laughed.

He looked at his grandmother's pale face, and the rise and fall of her chest as she breathed. Then he glanced up at Melissa, bent over him in concern. Her face was also pale, her big eyes wide with their now-familiar anxious look. Gran and Melissa had both been hurt, but they were all right. They'd survived.

And so have I.

'Callum.'

257

Jacob was standing in the shattered doorway, still barred from entering the house. Callum smiled.

'Come in,' he said. 'Come in, Jacob. You are welcome here.'

The pale boy bowed politely. Then he stepped easily across the cottage threshold. He picked his way cautiously around the scattered rowan berries and came to stand by the fire, near Melissa and Callum.

'It is nice to be welcome,' he said.

'Should we call an ambulance?' asked Melissa.

Jacob knelt down beside Gran and held his hand over her head for a moment. His eyes closed, as if he was concentrating on a distant voice that only he could hear. Then, after a moment, they opened again.

'The old lady is not seriously hurt,' he declared.

'Thank God,' breathed Callum, his shoulders sagging with relief.

'But shouldn't she see a doctor, just in case?' asked Melissa.

'If I were you, I would leave things be,' replied Jacob. 'Doctors will have too many questions that you cannot answer. She is strong and proud, this one. She will not thank you if she wakes to find strangers fussing over her. '

'That's true,' said Callum. 'I suppose we'd better clear this up, though,' he added, bending down to pick up pieces of broken crockery.

'Let me help,' offered Melissa.

'You'll just make it worse!'

This time they laughed together.

'You stay there. Just stay by Gran and keep an eye on her. I'll clean up. I know where everything goes.' Callum thought of Gran's saying: *As long as everything is in its right place, there's plenty of room.*

The worst part was the broken glass door. Callum went to the kitchen for a broom and swept all the glass out on to the patio – there wasn't much to see there any more. There was no sign of Doom, nor of the body of the Fetch. A makeshift DIY job of nailing a blanket over the gaping hole cut out a bit of the cold. Finally, Callum cleared up the broken crockery and swept the debris into the bin under the sink in the kitchen.

Jacob and Melissa watched Callum work, neither of them speaking. Callum realised with a twist of apprehension in his heart that they were waiting for him to tell them their next moves. They wanted him to act as their leader.

For a moment, when he came back to the sitting room, Callum simply stood looking at his strange new friends – one dead, one living, both of them far more complex than he had ever guessed.

Both of them were worth having on his side.

'So what happens now?' Callum demanded softly. 'Jacob, you're the one with all the answers. What comes next? How many more creatures of the Netherworld will turn up on my doorstep?'

The unpredictable blood began to drip from Jacob's hands. He turned and held his hands up to the fire, as if he were warming them, until the dark rivulets dried and disappeared. He spoke with his back to Callum.

'I don't know what manner of being will come next,' Jacob answered quietly. Even muted, his voice rang like the striking of a muffled bell. 'The Fetch has been defeated; one threat against your life has been thwarted. The threat of the Shadowing is about to begin. One Churchyard Grim will not protect you, or your world, from all the Netherworld breaking its boundaries and overwhelming it with darkness.'

Callum hesitated. Melissa sat with her head bent, one hand on Gran's forehead, listening but keeping her mouth shut. Another thing she was good at, Callum realised: knowing when to stand back.

'What will?' Callum asked. 'Tell me what *will* protect my world.'

'You.'

'How can I help?'

'Fight with me. Fight to keep the boundary intact. I know you feel you didn't ask for this –'

'I didn't ask for it,' Callum interrupted. 'But who asks for anything they're born with – the colour of their skin, their parents, the place they live? You're stuck with what you get. You've got to make the most of it.'

'For yourself, if for no one else,' Melissa repeated. 'It's worth fighting for yourself.'

'And you, and Gran.'

'And Ed,' Melissa pointed out softly.

Callum took a breath. He nodded. 'Yeah. People

confused about who their real enemies are.'

'It is hard to tell, sometimes,' Jacob said. He was still holding his hands up to the fire, and didn't look at Callum as he spoke. 'When your enemy has the same face as your friend. Well . . .'

'But you're right,' said Callum. 'I have to help. I'll fight with you.'

Melissa rolled her eyes. 'That's what I've been saying all along.'

Gran suddenly moaned and rubbed her forehead. Melissa bent over her in concern. 'Mrs Scott? Mrs Scott?' she said. 'Can you hear me?' She shifted the cushion beneath Gran's head and smoothed back the short grey hair.

'I think she's waking up,' Melissa said to Callum.

Callum knelt by Melissa's side, frowning with worry as he watched Gran stirring restlessly. Her eyes still closed, the old woman rolled away from Melissa and moaned again.

Jacob stood up. 'I must go. Doom is finished out there, and we have no more business in your house tonight.'

'When will I see you again?' Callum asked.

'If you need me, if you need anything, you know where to find me. But perhaps' – Jacob gave his wistful smile – 'perhaps there will be a brief time for us both to rest, before the Shadowing is upon us.' He nodded to Melissa. 'Translator, you will be welcome too. With or without the chime child. Thank you.'

Melissa stared at the ghost, surprise showing in her big eyes. 'What for?'

For the first time, Jacob's voice was so quiet it didn't echo.

'You aren't afraid of me,' he said. 'You never were.'

'I'll go with you,' said Melissa softly. 'At least, I mean I'll leave now too. Give Callum and his gran some peace, I think.'

Jacob crossed the room to the door and waited. After an awkward few seconds Callum realised that he was waiting for someone to open the door for him.

'Can't you just float through?' he asked, only half joking.

'Not this door,' Jacob said. 'Your grandmother has it wreathed with spells.'

Callum held the door open for Jacob and Melissa. On the front path, Doom sat waiting, silent and still.

'There you go.'

Jacob faced Callum.

'Tell me to leave. You should not allow any spirit free access to your home. If I come back, you may invite me in again.'

Callum grinned. 'Leave my house,' he ordered. 'And don't darken this doorstep again.'

Jacob's pale features relaxed into his faint smile. Callum smiled back. Then Jacob bowed, just as he'd done before entering. He stepped over the threshold and into the night, Melissa walking at his side. But Jacob turned back to Callum once more.

'One final thing, Callum. Do not tell your grandmother about me.'

'Why not?'

'Imagine how she'll react if you tell her a ghost has penetrated all her magical barriers and entered her cottage! I didn't do anything to defeat the Fetch; you and Melissa and Doom did all the battling yourselves. Leave me out of the story.' Jacob paused. 'Besides, women don't like to think about lost children. It makes them sad.'

Jacob's eyes began to leak the strange, black blood, like dark tears glistening on his white cheeks in the moonlight.

'Farewell, Callum,' he said. 'Until our next meeting.'

Then the ghost and the black dog slowly faded from view, leaving Melissa standing by herself in the empty garden, quiet in the moonlight. Nothing told of the last hour's terror and struggle against the Netherworld, except perhaps the open gate: a boundary waiting to be crossed.

The time of the Shadowing was about to begin.

Melissa walked out on to the lane and closed the gate firmly behind her.

'*We'll* meet again on Monday morning,' she said firmly. 'At school.'

'See you,' Callum said, and watched her set off fearlessly up the moonlit road through Marlock Wood.

Callum turned back to the brightly lit cottage and shut the door. Gran was sitting up, one hand to her head, frowning a little.

'What am I doing on the floor?' she asked crossly. 'Oh, Callum, what's happened to your face!'

'Gran!' Callum cried out with relief, and ran to her.

'That thing –' Gran reached towards Callum with both arms. 'Did that monster do that to you – is it here?' She looked around wildly.

'No, Gran, no,' Callum said, kneeling by her side and putting an arm around her shoulder. 'We destroyed it. We're safe.'

'Safe!' Gran repeated incredulously. She looked Callum in the eye, their faces close together, understanding. 'We're not safe.'

'We're safe tonight,' Callum assured her. 'But you're right, Gran. The Shadowing is about to begin.'

Then he added with fierce determination, 'And I'm going to beat it.'

Epilogue

The room is dark, but for the open fire. Alone and pacing before the flames, a man waits. Everything about him is restless. He runs his hands through his hair, then crosses his arms and sighs. He stamps one foot as he pivots, back and forth, back and forth, up and down the dark room. Every now and then he stares intensely at the fire. Seeing nothing, he continues his relentless pacing.

Up and down the room. Another sigh. Another glance at the fire.

The man stops. Suddenly, in the flames, he sees the sign he is watching for. The fire has changed. Its flames have turned violet – a bright, cold, blue-purple, the colour of black light. The white cuff at the man's wrist and the jewel set in his ring glow unnaturally in the strange light. Everything else is cast into darkness.

In the depths of the blue and purple flames, a face appears. Its features are all wrong – ruby-red eyes too far apart to be human, the pupils slitted like a goat's, pointed teeth that are pitted like pumice stone.

The man nods to the evil face. It is a greeting. He shows no sign of fear or surprise that a monster has appeared in his fire. This is what he was expecting, what he has been waiting for. But he is fearful about what he has to report to the demonic face. He is the bearer of bad news.

The demon's voice is like the hiss of water thrown into a blaze.

'Well?'

The man answers reluctantly. 'Our assassin has been destroyed.'

'How so?'

'A Grim.'

The demon's features writhe. Having no visible

body to shrug its shoulders with, it shows its indifference with a twist of its mouth.

'One Fetch matters little,' the demon spits. 'It was a vain and shallow creature. *The Hunter!* But it has performed its task well. The chime children are dead and still the mortals live in ignorance of the shadow realm, imagining its beings are merely the stuff of folk tale and nightmare.

'When the Shadowing comes,' the creature continues, 'and the boundaries are open, with the chime children gone there will be no resistance to our army. We will fix the gateways between the worlds so that they will remain open forever. The realm of mortals will be ours for the taking.'

The man shifts uncomfortably on his feet, his hands behind his back, like a soldier facing a superior officer.

'Not all the chime children have been slain,' he reveals.

The demon pauses dangerously.

'How many remain?'

The man hesitates.

'One.'

The demon laughs, a sound of spitting sparks, like drops of water sizzling in hot oil.

'One!' The glowing red eyes crinkle with amusement. 'One!' The demon howls with laughter again. 'What is *one?* Rest easy, friend. One chime child against all the demon force of the Netherworld? They will be as a pebble before the tide.'

The demon's laughter dies away.

'Prepare yourself. We are coming.'

Turn over if you dare for a chilling preview of the second book in the series . . .

THE SHADOWING
SKINNED

There aren't any trees in the little circular cul-de-sac where the boy lives, but there is a tall, wooden telephone pole, sprouting a wire into each house in the street. Every night before bed, the boy checks to see if there are any birds roosting on the wire that ties the pole to his own house. Sometimes on winter nights there are stars between the cables. Tonight there is a full moon. The boy leans his elbows on the windowsill and stares, imagining flying off in a spaceship.

Then, suddenly, the night twists.

It is the weirdest thing the boy has ever seen. The view from his window warps for a moment, as though it's reflected in a wobbly mirror from a funfair. For a second, the air between the cable and the ground seems to break and reform, the way still water ripples when you touch it.

The boy rubs his eyes. He shakes his head before he looks again to see if the ripple is still there.

It isn't. Instead, there is a woman standing on the pavement.

Before the air rippled, before the boy rubbed his eyes, no one had been there. Now there is a strange woman. Above the mysterious figure, caught between the stretching cables, the full moon hangs in the sky. In its pale light, the woman's skin is faintly blue, as though she has been nearly frozen to death. Around her shoulders is a tattered shawl, too full of holes to protect against the winter air. Her ragged leather skirt doesn't look very warm, either.

Where did she come from? An empty street, a ripple in the air, and now this ice-blue woman.

The boy at the window is fascinated. He can't look away.

*

Black Annis lifts her head, searching one way and then the other. Above her stands a wooden mast with thick, black ropes stretching out to the strange houses around it. Beneath her feet, the ground is as hard as rock and as smooth as eggshell.

The world has changed.

When last she walked this land, it was field and forest. Now all that is gone. Tree and hedgerow gone. No trees anywhere — only this bare wooden pole. Gone, too, the place Black Annis lived, the cave she scratched from the sandstone of Dane's Hill with her own nails. Gone, the oak that grew at its mouth, where she hung out the flayed skins of her victims to dry so that later she might sew them for her skirts.

What is that smell — thick and acrid? It surrounds her, dulling the cold, fresh scent of night and the aroma of warm, living things. All changed, all gone — nothing remains of Black Annis's world. It is buried beneath this grey layer of grit and tar, and row upon row of smoky human dwellings. For a moment, in the cavity where her shrivelled, inhuman heart beats, Black Annis knows something like despair.

Then her eyes follow one of the black ropes overhead. It stretches from the top of the tall, wooden pole to the bottom of a window. And in the window, moonlight shining on his white face, there is a child.

Black Annis smiles. Her pointed teeth do not gleam in the moonlight; they are black with age and the bloodstains of her countless victims. Her teeth are as strong and sharp as her nails. She looks up at the human child – surely meant to be in bed and asleep at this time of night.

Some things don't change.

*

The boy watches as the cold woman turns her head, looking up at the telephone pole, and finally looking at him. Straight at him. Her eyes seem alight, shining silver in the moonlight. Her lips pull back over teeth that make a dark stain in the middle of her pale, bluish face.

It is a smile. She sees him.

Now he notices something else. Her arms seem too long for her body, and her fingers – no one can have fingers that long! Unless . . . Can they be her *fingernails?*

The boy snaps out of his trance, all fascination instantly turned to fear. He backs away from the window.

*

Black Annis walks towards the house. Inside the gate, separating the house from the hard grey ground beyond, there is a tiny patch of grass and earth. The soil here is something else that has not changed. The sandy loam is soft and familiar. It is good to feel the earth beneath her feet again.

Black Annis reaches the house and looks up. It is bigger than the human dwelling places she remembers. The windows are higher.

But her nails are as sharp as ever they were. She is good at climbing.

*

Cowering away from the window, the boy can see nothing. But he can hear an odd noise outside – a scratching beneath the window, growing steadily louder. The boy doesn't want to look, but he has to know what it is.

He forces himself back to the window. He grips the sill and peers out across the street. The strange woman is gone.

But the noise is still growing louder. The boy looks down at the window ledge outside the house. Long, iron claws are hooked into the wood. As the boy watches, the dark claws flex and grip. Behind them rise long, pale arms, blue in the moonlight. The arms haul up the rest of the weird body. Black teeth and silver eyes rise into view, filling the window.

*

Black Annis is face-to-face with her victim. Her grin widens. The human child throws himself into his bed and dives under the covers. Black Annis can see the heap of human helplessness trembling beneath the flimsy cloth and down.

The boy's terror is delicious.

*

Under his duvet, the boy hides, his nerves a snarled tangle of despair and hope. Surely he is safe here. The blue woman can't see him any more, and the window is shut tight –

Click

The sound is soft and sudden. A cold draught of night air reaches under the covers and caresses the boy's trembling ankles. The window is open.

The child waits, his heart pounding with terror, as he listens to the quiet, slow footfalls padding across his bedroom floor.

There is no more warning. The covers are ripped from his body in one lightning sweep. It is too late for him to scream for help.

He screams anyway.

A breathless action thriller
with a brand new hero: Jake Bastin is . . .

STRIKER
NICK HALE

'Practically impossible to put down'

STRIKER

THE EDGE

NICK HALE

ISBN: 978 1 4052 5685 8

Jake Bastin can't believe he's been scouted for Olympic Advantage. It's a dream come true to train with the top teenage athletes from around the world . . .

But the sunny Florida camp is hiding a nasty secret. Painkillers are being issued illegally and many of the athletes are getting seriously aggressive. Jake knows something is up, and he's in the perfect position to report back to MI6.

It's his first mission on his own. Popov will be watching . . .

International football meets the world of espionage
and counter-terrorism in a nail-biting action thriller.

IT'S A BRAVE NEW WORLD

MIKE LANCASTER

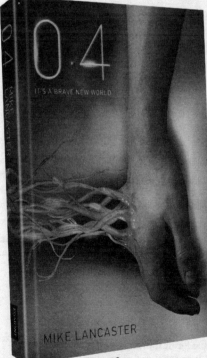

'My name is Kyle Straker.
And I don't exist any more.'

So begins the story of Kyle Straker,
recorded on old audio tapes.

You might think these tapes are a
hoax. But perhaps they contain the
history of a past world . . .

If what the tapes say are true,
it means that everything we think we
know is a lie.

And if everything is a lie does that
mean that we are, too?

ISBN: 978 1 4052 5304 8

*Plug into a gripping new
generation of sci-fi*

EGMONT PRESS: ETHICAL PUBLISHING

Egmont Press is about turning writers into successful authors and children into passionate readers – producing books that enrich and entertain. As a responsible children's publisher, we go even further, considering the world in which our consumers are growing up.

Safety First
Naturally, all of our books meet legal safety requirements. But we go further than this; every book with play value is tested to the highest standards – if it fails, it's back to the drawing-board.

Made Fairly
We are working to ensure that the workers involved in our supply chain – the people that make our books – are treated with fairness and respect.

Responsible Forestry
We are committed to ensuring all our papers come from environmentally and socially responsible forest sources.

For more information, please visit our website at
www.egmont.co.uk/ethical

Egmont is passionate about helping to preserve the world's remaining ancient forests. We only use paper from legal and sustainable forest sources, so we know where every single tree comes from that goes into every paper that makes up every book.

This book is made from paper certified by the Forestry Stewardship Council (FSC), an organisation dedicated to promoting responsible management of forest resources. For more information on the FSC, please visit **www.fsc.org**. To learn more about Egmont's sustainable paper policy, please visit **www.egmont.co.uk/ethical**.